LATENCY

HUNTER BUREAU #2

BLAZE WARD

KNOTTED ROAD PRESS

Additional Alexandria Station Stories

Siren

Two Bottles of Wine with a War God

The Story Road

The Science Officer Series

The Science Officer

The Mind Field

The Gilded Cage

The Pleasure Dome

The Doomsday Vault

The Last Flagship

The Hammerfield Gambit

The Hammerfield Payoff

Shadow of the Dominion

Longshot Hypothesis

Hard Bargain

Outermost

Dominion-427

Phoenix

Princess Rualoh

Latency
Hunter Bureau #2
Blaze Ward
Copyright © 2020 Blaze Ward
All rights reserved
Published by Knotted Road Press
www.KnottedRoadPress.com

ISBN: 978-1-64470-177-5

Cover art:

ID 131408614 © Andrey Golubtsov | Dreamstime.com
ID 86344101 © Ilya Shalkov | Dreamstime.com

Cover and interior design copyright © 2020 Knotted Road Press

Reviews
It's true. Reviews help. Even a short one, such as, "Loved it!" So please consider reviewing this book (and all of the ones you've read) on your favorite retailer site.

Never miss a release!
If you'd like to be notified of new releases, sign up for my newsletter.

http://www.blazeward.com/newsletter/

Buy More!
Did you know that you can buy directly from my website?

https://www.blazeward.com/shop/

[1]
BANG

Lunch time. Nice day downtown not too far from Boston Common. Sidewalk café on the ground floor of one of those towers that had gone up after the aliens arrived and changed everything.

Just sitting and shooting the breeze with Rachel Asher.

Greyson was still getting used to having a partner again. He'd been retired for over a year, and had mostly worked solo before that.

Being a Detective/Hunter for the Earth Police Special Missions Hunter Bureau wasn't like a normal cop job. He wasn't out solving crimes most of the time, running down leads and stuff like that.

Sure, he did it. Maintained a quiet network of informants and criminal friends he could lean on in a pinch, but most of what the Hunters did involved death. Other departments, other agencies, would do all the legwork, but when things got ugly or tight then folks like Greyson got called into the picture.

You could teach someone how to be a cop. How to be a detective. Forensics and all the technical stuff.

You couldn't teach *Killer*. Folks were either born with it or they weren't. Trying to make someone a killer when they didn't have it in them ended up just breaking them after a while.

It had taken years for the brass to grasp that, but they'd finally given up on the psychological manipulation crap in training and started looking for people willing and able to put a beam weapon to an intelligent person's head—or more specifically an alien's—and pull the trigger.

Those people were mercifully few, but that was what the Hunters did. Most of the time, the beam was even on a heavy stun setting, so the Hunter could take that rogue alien in and question them. Palmstunners and the like. Safe enough to use, even in crowd situations, since you could sort everyone out and apologize later as necessary.

Every cop on the street was issued a palmstunner. Even Greyson had one, tucked under his belt on the right side, under the light jacket he wore when working. The kind of jacket that went with comfortable slacks and a nice-enough shirt. Greyson had ceremonially burned all his ties when he'd been fired the first time and he really didn't care enough to replace them. The brass got him like this and liked it, or they could go piss up a rope and he'd go back to his various pensions. His synth whiskey and his classical music. Noodles at the place down around the corner because the owner kept prices cheap and Greyson could live small.

He didn't need to be a cop.

They'd needed him to come back into the fold, not the other way around.

Greyson looked across the lunch table at his partner. Rachel Asher. Kid young enough to be one of his, if he'd had any he knew about. Another killer. Patrolman/Hunter on her way to making Detective and then Brass one of these days, except that she wasn't staying in Boston to do it.

Eventually, Scotland Yard would open a slot for her to take a lateral and she'd become a Bobby. Or something. Probably three days after she completed that law degree she was constantly studying towards.

Like now. Head down with a cup of coffee in her off hand. Nose in a tablet reading homework. That book reader was even more reliable than her shoes.

Rachel had stopped wearing a tie after she got paired with him. Greyson figured he was a bad influence on the kid, but he didn't care. She was a good cop. Would be better than him once she learned a few more things, and then she'd move into one of those corner offices with a view of a river somewhere.

If he wasn't already pushing fifty, he'd maybe consider transferring to London when she did, just so he could have her as a boss. Greyson Leigh hadn't learned anything about Rachel to convince him that would be a bad turnabout.

Her eyes came up just enough to confirm that he was staring at her.

Cop sense.

She had it.

Rachel started to say something and a sound interrupted. Short. Loud. Sharp. Over.

Three bangs.

"What the hell?" she asked, but Greyson was already on his feet and moving. He paused just long enough to drop enough cash to cover lunch on the table and he was sprinting away.

Firefighters run to the sound of trouble.

Cops run towards gunfire.

Chemically-propelled slugthrowers, using gunpowder, were illegal anywhere except a dedicated facility, after a long process before you could get all the necessary permits. It was an expensive hobby Greyson had never felt the need to indulge in, unlike some other cops who yearned for a forgotten silver age of cowboys and indians.

And a few hard-case criminals who liked things that went bang.

He considered drawing his palmstunner, but decided that whoever it was shooting things was already trouble with *Poor Impulse Control* tattooed across his forehead. And they were still firing, so people were at risk.

He reached under his left arm and pulled out the Nerve Scrambler.

Only Hunters were issued these weapons. They could take down anybody at short range, up to and including a Phrenic, those brutally-efficient shapeshifters that had to wear a suppressor device if they didn't want to be arrested on sight.

Or killed.

More gunfire. Three slower shots. Greyson was back in the army again. Back in the early Twenty-first Century. Before the aliens came and made the world over. Back when violence was used to solve problems.

Boston was a hard town, but it had adapted well to peaceful times. The sidewalk was a little crowded with people frantically running for cover in buildings or behind anything heavy enough to stop a bullet.

Midday. Spring wasn't that far off, so he'd settled for just the jacket and not anything heavier. Most of his work was indoors or riding in a car, but a sidewalk café had been a good idea. Out in the sun and nice breeze, after a winter cooped up.

It still snowed in the winter in Boston many years. Not as bad as when he'd been a kid, to say nothing of his grandparents, who had stories of blizzards so bad the city came to a halt for a week.

Nice enough day, but for some punk with an illegal gun taking pot shots at the world.

There.

Greyson found the center of the maelstrom as people were all headed outward from a single point. Of course, this moron had walked into a small park today and decided to open fire.

At least the shooter was outside, where someone like Greyson Leigh might hear him, rather than confined in a building, where he could barricade himself in and nobody would know until a victim managed to trigger a panic button.

Male. Ragged but middle-class, with a slight paunch and clothes that he hadn't gotten second hand. Several days stubble on the side of the chin Greyson could see from here. Almost looked like an accountant who had suffered a psychotic break.

He was reloading. Damn, was that a flipping revolver? Where the hell had he stolen a relic like that?

Greyson's grandfather had had something like that, demilled when the aliens decided to make humans safer. It couldn't fire. The one over there did.

Greyson counted three bodies down and ignored the wild screaming sounds from the other survivors, all fleeing for their lives, so that he wasn't distracted.

He knew the range of the nerve scrambler. That hand cannon had a longer reach, but Greyson was quiet. He slowed and realized that Rachel had been silently pacing him, even with her stubbier legs and heavy boots.

She had her nerve scrambler out, too. Probably had no idea what Greyson was up to and just being careful and paranoid.

"Police, drop the weapon!" Greyson yelled as he came down to a jog at the edge of deadly range.

Never stop moving with a shooter, so you can dodge suddenly, but take the time to be careful.

And not everyone knows what a Hunter is, so the sound of his voice would likely just draw fire. It was possible though, that identifying himself as a simple cop would break through to the man. Or draw fire this way.

Nobody wore the sorts of Kevlar vests Greyson had lived in as a soldier, so he was just as at risk as everyone else in view.

The bastard with the illegal hand cannon merely snapped the cylinder shut and turned his way, raising it.

In all the movies, the cops always managed to avoid being shot at fifteen meters by a maniac with a gun like that. They had to take that moment to let the audience know that they were the good guys and had no choice but to take the bad guy down, but only *after* lives were at risk.

Greyson shot the fucker dead center and drove hard to his right with a planted foot, just to get away from that questing barrel.

Nerve scrambler was one hell of a rude weapon. Against humans, generally terminal, unless someone just got brushed by the edge of the field or was out at the edge of effective range.

There was a hospital close enough to treat someone who'd been hammered. Save his life, maybe, in some sort of medical miracle.

Greyson shot him again as the first bolt drove the man to his knees.

Rachel followed with a shot of her own, but Greyson had already seen the light go out in the man's eyes.

Dead.

No longer a threat to Hunters or innocent civilians just running errands on their lunch hour.

He was still jogging, so he circled farther right and closed with the man.

"Call for backup and medical emergencies," Greyson turned to Rachel with a hard face.

She was a little green around the gills, but nodded and pulled out her Communicator. She stopped moving before she stepped in a blood puddle.

Greyson always owned pants that blood would wash out of.

Potential victims were still running, so Greyson had the entire space to himself right now. Just him, Rachel, the dead guy, and a handful of victims.

He approached with the nerve scrambler all set for a fourth bolt if the corpse sat up right now.

Greyson still had weird nightmares that he didn't dare talk about with the Bureau shrinks, lest they start asking harder questions and maybe take him in for a battery of tests that might get him killed.

Like how he had survived being shot with a similar weapon while hunting a Phrenic through the catacombs under Boston last fall. Or the fact that he was a Phrenic himself, a frightened being buried so deeply into the personality of Greyson Leigh that neither of them understood where one ended and the other started.

Except that Greyson was in command of their body. Ethen had retreated to a little box in a closet, up on the shelf in back, where Greyson's mind could protect him from the universe.

Rachel suspected the truth, but had never said anything to anyone, or they would have shot him on sight.

He was still Greyson Leigh, regardless of the body he wore. Cop. Hunter.

Killer.

The shooter was dead.

Nerve scrambler three times dead.

Not-fucking-around dead.

Greyson scanned the space for any other shooters. Seeing none, he holstered his nerve scrambler and gingerly picked up the revolver by the end of the barrel. Then dropped it because he'd forgotten how hot those damned things got.

After putting gloves on, he tried a second time, muttering curses at himself.

Wow. Museum piece Ruger. 1970s model, give or take. Back when that one actor had made them the gun every fool had to have for protection. Including Greyson's grandfather.

Blue steel .44 Magnum. In those days, it really had been the most powerful handgun on Earth and take your head clean off.

Those days were past. And guns like this were illegal as anything outside of a licensed gun range with really high annual dues and a crap-ton of paperwork on file.

Who the hell was this man, that he'd even had access to something like that? And what would cause a middle-aged accountant, maybe ten years older than Greyson from the thinning hair turning white and the lines around the eyes and mouth, to just walk into a park and start shooting people?

Clothes screamed middle-class office drone. Accountant or actuary. Something bland and forgettable. Maybe off-the-rack wool in charcoal tailored by an expert, rather than bespoke.

"Company inbound," Rachel said as she stepped close. "I let them know we were here and things were calm, so they didn't arrive shooting. Unlike someone I know."

He glanced over but she was grinning. That was good. Anything else and she'd have gotten the sharp side of his tongue.

He wasn't a cop, but Hunters were still the people who ran towards gunfire.

"Hey, what's that?" she asked suddenly, kneeling next to the dead guy.

Unlike him, she already had her gloves on, but she was still closer to police academy.

He'd been a professional assassin for the US Army at her age. Cop only happened later.

Greyson stepped around so he didn't shade her from the bright sun that had suddenly come out from behind the clouds.

Rachel reached into her jacket pocket and pulled out a knife. Long and straight like a stiletto. Useful tool.

She prodded at something on the side of the guy's head, right behind his left ear.

Greyson had never gone in for one of those data-jacks that had become all the rage after the aliens first arrived on Earth sixteen years ago. Sure, you could plug your brain straight into a global communications network and have access to a galactic encyclopedia of information, sports, and entertainment.

But Rachel wasn't old enough to know what a modal popup window was. Or why it might never go away if the programmer behind it was enough of an asshole. Especially the ones who played a stupid pop song from the 1980s.

Yeah, I'm going to give you up, fucker.

"What have you got?" he asked anyway, in case it hadn't been what it seemed.

"Synth Chip," Rachel replied, leaving it in place, plugged into the guy's skull like a dongle in a USB port. Another reference she might be too young to get. "The name on it is *Killer.*"

She turned a confused look up at him.

"I thought that Synth Chips were supposed to override

everything, so you sat quietly in a chair and lived whatever experience was programmed into them?" she asked/said.

Like him, she wasn't jacked. If you wanted that level of immersion, there were places you could go where they would suit you up and put a helmet on you, invoking it all through a *SQUID*. A *Superconducting QUantum Interface Device*.

Beam crap straight into your brain, but do it through your skull.

For a lot of people, it was just way easier to get a data-jack and plug things right into your mind.

Greyson had never wanted one. Greyson in Ethen's mesomorphed body couldn't have one, because neither of them was sure what a medical scanner would show.

"That's the theory," Greyson said. "Something obviously went wrong with this one. Whatever homicide detective gets the case will have fun sorting it out."

"They won't assign us?" she asked. "We were here."

"We're Hunters, Rachel," Greyson said as cops in Skycruisers started dropping out of the sky with lights flashing and sirens wailing.

He had the revolver by the barrel still, but held it at arm's length, just so no punk with a twitchy finger stunned him right now.

In about thirty seconds, none of this would be his problem anyway.

2

DETECTIVE/CAPTAIN

THE SHOOTING HAD BEEN ALL OVER THE NEWS RACHEL had been watching for two days now, but like Leigh had said, it had been handed off to some homicide detective as fast as one could arrive and be briefed. They'd gone back to the restaurant, had dessert, and disappeared. Thinking that they were done.

Apparently, she'd been wrong.

Rachel looked up from her homework now as the door opened and Captain Parsons looked out at her and Greyson in the two seats, like truant school kids sent to sit outside the principal's office. Parsons was an English word that always conjured up images of a lean, fussy, Anglican priest on a rolling, green wilderness, playing religious music on an old-fashioned organ.

This woman had none of that going.

Parsons was maybe five eight in bare feet, plus five inches of heels going today. Bottle blond who took the time to touch up her roots but not her brunette eyebrows. Blue eyes in that Slavic way from so many who had come over to

North America over the last three generations. Cheek bones a girl could shave her legs with in a pinch.

Absolute trouble.

"Both of you," Captain said in a voice tinged with an even mix of vitriol and bile, like the world's meanest martini.

Rachel slid her reader into the outside pocket of her jacket and followed Greyson into the office. He didn't give two shits about much of anything, but Leigh was like that. He'd been ousted from the Bureau a year and a half ago when his investigations into smuggling and corruption got a little too close to the former incumbent of this office, that asshole Zielinski.

Detective/Captain Rutherford Parsons. Weird name to hang on a daughter, but the woman was most definitely woman. Political operative of the kind who swam with big sharks. Tall, but every woman felt tall compared to Rachel's five foot two. Bustier, or maybe just not strapping them down to fit under body armor, like folks in the field did.

Folks other than Greyson. He never wore armor of any kind. Again, no shits to give. Plus, Rachel was pretty sure shooting the man would just piss him off.

Parsons was an outsider in the Boston office. Lots of folks had suddenly taken a quiet retirement and fled to places like Florida and Buenos Aires when Zielinski got tossed out on his ass last fall. One Detective/Sergeant had stayed and made it to Detective/Lieutenant. All the rest of the brass, and anybody with stripes, were new.

This woman had been transferred over from the Los Angeles office of the Bureau when she got promoted to Captain.

Like Leigh, she didn't give two shits about the folks left behind when a third of them were at least *suspected* of being dirty.

Rachel hadn't been around long enough to develop any

really bad habits from men like Dominguez or Kovalchuk. They were both dead now, or else they would probably also be learning a new language on the fly themselves.

Wherever was far enough to hide from jurisdiction and extradition. Parsons had eventually concluded that out of sight would be enough not to warrant further investigations.

This office had been dirty. Rachel knew that now. Too many corrupt little gigs on the side, bringing in enough cash that Dominguez had had a couple of years' worth of salary tied up just in the bespoke suits in his closet.

Rachel was really glad some of the incorruptibleness of Greyson Leigh was rubbing off on her. That would look good on her next job application.

London.

Couple more years to her degree. Then she'd see.

Assuming she made it out of this office alive and employed in the next thirty minutes.

Parsons had suddenly changed into someone else when the door clicked shut. Friendly, but Rachel couldn't actually imagine what unfriendlier might look like. Less likely—maybe—to rip one of their heads off, literally.

Rachel slipped into the far chair and let the Captain face Leigh.

Match made in hell, as long as she didn't have to oust the Devil when she got there.

"You shot the man with a nerve scrambler," Parsons said in a tired, ragged voice that sounded like she'd been screaming at a stupid reporter on the phone.

Walls were soundproof. Might have happened while Rachel was reading English Jurisprudence.

"He was reloading an illegal firearm, having already shot and killed three innocent victims who randomly happened to be in his way," Leigh growled back.

Like maybe the two of them already had this discussion once when she wasn't around.

What had she missed in the last two days?

They'd handed off to Metro PD, been interviewed, thanked by the Detectives on the scene for controlling things quickly, then sent on their way. Right?

"You carry a palmstunner for a reason, Leigh," Parsons replied in an exhausted, grumpy voice.

"Sure," he said. "When there's a chance that the person I'm shooting is innocent and this is all just a terrible misunderstanding that can be worked out."

Rachel wondered if she'd be without a partner again in about five minutes, given the look on Parsons's face.

Parsons flexed her neck and shoulders in such a way that suggested someone was holding it in a big, invisible mitt right now, then she reached out a hand tipped with delicate, red-tipped nails. Like she'd dipped them in the blood of her most recent victim. The woman pulled a file and flipped it open.

"So you didn't know that a palmstunner would have no effect on the target?" she asked, suddenly innocent and bright in a whipsawing kind of way.

Rachel blinked. Leigh didn't even twitch.

"Sure, we'll go with that," he said in a *whatever* kind of voice.

"Or didn't care?" Parsons asked.

Leigh smiled grimly. He was like that at least half the time.

But weren't they all, at some level?

"Metro PD has asked for you to be assigned to the case, Leigh," Parsons said in a voice without an opinion on the topic.

That got Greyson leaning forward. Rachel found herself mirroring her partner's body language.

What the hell?

She'd have said something instead of thinking it really loudly, but the Captain was having a conversation with Leigh right now. The *shut-up-and-learn-something-rookie* kind of conversation.

Rachel watched instead.

"Hunter Bureau deals with alien issues, Captain Parsons," Leigh said unequivocally.

"Lucky for me, then, that I have an expert on the topic at hand, isn't it?" the Captain smiled and closed the trap around the man's leg as Rachel marveled at the setup. "The Synch Chip was an alien design. Alien manufacture. Alien issue."

"The guy was human," Leigh countered, a little less sure now, like he could feel those steel jaws poised to draw blood.

Rachel sure felt them, but she was only chained to the victim, as near as she could tell. There was still a chance she might escape intact without having to gnaw her leg off first. Because Parsons—and whoever was pulling her chain—was looking like they were trying to get on Leigh's nerves. That would be bad.

While there were more dangerous things in the galaxy than having Greyson Leigh hunting you, those weren't survivable, either.

"He was," Parsons smiled now with those Slavic cheekbones and glacial blue eyes. "Someone designed that chip for a human, with an override in place that didn't cut out all his muscles when he was in that fantasy projection as is legally required. Your victim slotted it in and thought he was running a sim that let him act out the role of a serial killer from the safety of his own flat. Palmstunner might have tickled him. Might not. Would have set up the first cop coming along to get his fool head blown off. But someone took him down with a nerve scrambler instead."

Rachel felt her eyes want to go big but concentrated on

looking as gruff and jaded as Leigh habitually did. She doubted that Parsons was fooled. Greyson certainly wasn't, but it would be good practice on civilians when she needed it.

Leigh shrugged.

"So why does Metro PD want me on the case?" he asked finally. "Not my specialty. Not even remotely my jurisdiction, unless someone's pulling strings to get me involved."

"Oh, you're already involved, Leigh," Parsons smiled and the jaws closed that last little bit. "I just got off the phone with the *Metropolitan*. The Honorable Denise Upkins herself. She's the one requesting and pulling strings."

"Why?" he countered in a hard tone Rachel identified as cop-voice.

"The victim/perp had a picture of you in his pocket when you took him down, Leigh," Parsons smile turned deadly serious. "Your face. Your name. Your bullseye."

Rachel couldn't help the profanity that slipped out of her mouth.

Somebody—maybe several somebodies—was going to die for this. She knew Greyson Leigh well enough to understand that much.

Things were about to get ugly in this town.

3

COFFEE WITH A SIDE OF CONSPIRACY

GREYSON STRETCHED HIS BACK AND NECK AS HE WALKED into the sunlight outside the headquarters building, automatically checking the sky and confirming that it was a little past mid-morning.

There'd been a splash of rain while he was inside getting the shit dumped on him by Captain Parsons. Almost made the streets smell nice, until the breeze shifted and he was downwind of a dumpster somewhere. The kind that hadn't been emptied in a while.

Rachel tagged along, looking bright and intelligent and serious and whatever else.

He stopped walking and turned towards her. One hand went out and grabbed her jacket enough to hold her in place as the back of his other knuckles rapped on the armor plate she was wearing under her dress shirt, right over her breasts.

Thunk, thunk.

Good.

"Yeah?" she asked him in a sarcastic tone, grinning.

Sounded like a woman wondering if he was about to rip

all her clothes off right in public and have his way with her. She could be a goof when she wanted to.

The rumors around the office suggested that they had been more than job partners. Greyson hadn't done anything to dissuade those fools.

Anybody wanting to underestimate me, or her, go right ahead.

"Upgrade to a class four," Greyson said as he turned and started walking again. "Add the titanium plate that goes over your heart."

"You expecting the whole Bolivian Army, Butch?" she snarked.

"The whole Bolivian Army better be expecting me, Sundance," he fired back.

They were both single adults. She came over to his place every once in a while to talk cop shop and maybe watch old movies. They'd have a little synth whiskey. Occasionally she'd bring takeout.

With the lights out so they could watch vids on a tablet, it would look remarkably like they'd gone to bed and were busy humping their brains out to any asshole cop parked down the block watching Greyson's curtains.

He'd fooled more than one of them that way. She was learning professional paranoia as well.

Greyson found the coffee shop back across an alley and around a corner. The kind that cops mentally knew about but rarely went to, because it didn't have a drive through and there were two others around here that did.

The place wasn't dead, but the only other person in here besides the tattooed kid behind the counter was a young woman sitting in the back corner with two tablets in front of her, highlighting and reading.

Another student like Rachel, from the looks of things. Never even glanced up.

He ordered and paid. Rachel did the same.

He'd broken her of the habit of flashing a badge and expecting free service. If this were a megacorp chain, he might think about it, but they were in a small shop that might be owned by the kid making espresso right now.

Greyson tossed an extra tip in the jar.

"Ready to talk?" she asked after they got their cups and settled kitty-corner from the other customer.

Away from eavesdroppers, at least the kind not relying on electronic gear.

Greyson reached into his inside pocket and pulled his comm. They reminded him of the old digital smart phones from when he was a kid. A little longer than his hand. Not quite as wide.

Physics was physics and humans had an expectation when it came to pockets. Rachel's reader was the next size up. Greyson's folding tablet, back in his apartment, was the size above that.

He had a bigger model on his desk in the office, when he needed to do paperwork.

Right now, he called up the file that had been assigned to him and Rachel while Parsons was busy ruining his day and overriding every dodge or trick he'd thrown at her trying to not get assigned this case. That woman at least had a much wider and more inventive vocabulary than Zielinski ever had, so some of the turns of phrase were new.

The end result was still the same.

He toggled into the evidence section and flipped through pictures until he found the one he had in mind. Rachel had learned patience, so she sat and sipped as he worked.

Greyson found the image he wanted. Opened it and zoomed a little. Laid the device on the table between them and spun it around for her to look at.

"Yup, that's you," she said with a quick nod and a

sarcastic tone. "You ever considered a trimmed beard? Would make you look like a professor or something."

"Don't start," he warned her without any fire.

She grinned. It was a fun game they played. Doubly so because it looked like flirting to an outsider across the room.

She knew his secrets. Maybe she was just watching until she needed to kill him, but maybe she was learning to be the best Hunter the Bureau had ever seen. Any Bureau, whatever they called it in other countries.

"Yeah, that's me," he agreed after a silent beat. "But there's a problem here."

She just glanced up at him with those expressive brown eyes.

Always let the suspect tell you more than he intended, just because you're happy to listen to him incriminate himself. Another lesson he'd taught her.

"That's the current picture from my personnel file," Greyson continued. "They took a new one for my ID when I came back because the previous one they had was from five or six years ago."

Those eyes got big for a moment before they settled back into calm.

"That's stupid," she muttered. "Triple cross?"

"How so?" he asked, just to see where cop logic and intuition had taken her.

"So let's assume they're aiming that perp at you personally," Rachel said quietly, tapping the tabletop with her off hand to count things. "And maybe he gets you with that stupid gun. Eventually someone takes him down and they find that picture. Someone recognizes where it comes from and knows we've got a leak inside the Bureau. A rogue. Now Internal Affairs comes into play rough and starts climbing up everyone's butts with a microscope, looking for whoever set you up. Makes no sense."

"Good at the first layer, Rachel," he agreed with a smile. "But you're assuming they're only after me."

"Who else?" she asked.

"So what happens when IA gets a little lusty in their investigations?" he asked.

"Shit comes apart and we get nothing done," Rachel growled. She stopped and blinked hard. "Crap. They're setting Parsons up, too?"

"That would be my read, kid," he said. "She let a few folks escape justice rather than subjecting the entire Eastern North America Division, Earth Police Special Missions, Hunter Bureau to a rigorous purging like maybe she should have. The woman's an outsider in Boston, so everything is already a little roiled. She's been trying to calm things instead. What if someone wants her to fail?"

"Who?" Rachel asked.

Greyson shrugged.

"That's the edge of where logic takes me with what's on the table," he said grimly. "She's got enemies. I've got enemies. Hell, by being my partner you've probably got enemies and just don't know it yet."

"So how do we flush them?" Rachel's eyes got hard.

"Dunno," he admitted. "We're investigating several crimes and conspiracies here, if I'm right. Need to dance carefully, rather than just charging in with a nerve scrambler and shooting some stupid bastard in the face."

She grinned.

"It's a useful reputation to have, when you need to be subtle, Rachel," he continued in a quieter tone.

"So we're back to your army days?" she pivoted on him.

Greyson felt a cloak of death close lightly around his shoulders.

At her age, he was working as an assassin for the US Army. Back when the US was a thing and had an army they liked to sic on weaker nations. Not every problem could be solved with an invasion. Sometimes they needed a knife in the dark.

So they sent in men and women like Greyson Leigh.

Find your target and out-think him. Figure out what his escape route would be when trouble comes, so you can treat it like a game trail and build yourself a blind to hunt from. Flush him with some fake attack and let him come running to you.

Onto your blade with a minimum of fuss.

Rachel knew more than her security clearance allowed, but she needed to know those things about him. And how to take advantage of his experience in a field she'd never pursued.

"Yeah," Greyson agreed. "Back to the assassin days. We're going to play fast, loose, and mean with the rules on this one. About the only person I trust in this situation is Metropolitan Upkins and a few people on her staff."

"Folks like Edgar Redhawk?" Rachel asked quietly, referring to the man who had once been Chief of Staff of the local bureau, before everything went to hell. Now, he was a hatchetman for the Metropolitan herself.

And about as dangerous as Greyson.

"Him and a few others who've been with Denise for a long time," Greyson agreed.

"Do I need to know your backstory with the Metropolitan?" Rachel asked. "Is she a target someone's going after through you, and Parsons is just collateral damage along the way?"

Greyson blinked in surprise, reconsidering.

"Maybe," he admitted. "Again, if they can burn me and then Parsons, it's possible that all that shit can be made to stick to her."

"So everyone on the damned planet might be after you on this one, Leigh?" Rachel growled.

"Worse," Greyson replied. "Remember, that chip was from off-planet. The whole galaxy might be out to get me."

[4]
DEALS

GREYSON CONSIDERED HIS PARKING KARMA AS HE AND Rachel walked away from the car and he chirped the locks. Someone had been signaling to pull out into traffic just as he was needing a place. Maybe the gods liked him today.

Or they were setting him up and wanted him looking the wrong way. Never take the gods of karma or good parking for granted.

They were across the street from Boston Common. The grass was finally green after the dry winter and the trees were starting bloom. Weather wasn't nice enough for many tourists or locals to be enjoying the open space, but there were a few around.

In the distance, he could see Carl and his infamous pastry stand, out in the middle where a cold breeze had nothing to block it. That man had the Common pretty much to himself today, which was how Carl liked it.

Greyson was headed the other way, Rachel walking beside him like a pit bull someone had forgotten to leash. He didn't mind her being a little protective. Just meant that she'd shoot at least as fast as he did if it came to trouble.

He paused to look at something in a window, using it to see if there were any breaks in the pattern of traffic around them. Nobody seemed to be paying attention, which was good.

"Bolivian Army hiding?" Rachel asked, glancing at him in the glass reflection.

"Probably inside in the food court," he grinned.

"Remind me to pack a tear gas grenade next time," she grinned back.

He shook his head and continued walking. Into the arcade, turn and immediately up the stairs.

Revolution Books was up here. Liz didn't believe in overlighting things. Swore all that extra light did bad things to the books and the humans, so the place was partly gloom.

Walking into a cave was how he occasionally thought of it.

Liz looked up as they came close.

"Hiya, Rachel," she called as the door beeped. "Twenty and Twenty-one came in yesterday."

"On duty today," Rachel replied as she followed him to the counter. "Might come by later."

Greyson noted that Liz hadn't said anything to him yet. Just sort of grinned at him.

Liz was a semi-reformed accountant who had seen the light of day and turned herself into a goth. Too hard edged to be a hippy, but that had probably been the other option for a woman her age, assuming that being born again was going to be too mundane for someone like Liz.

She was somewhere on the far, soft side of sixty. White hair, white makeup, black lips, and black leather jacket with strange designs and metal spikes on it. She'd had the place for at least the last ten years, occasionally filling in Greyson's book collection, and then later liquidating it when he downsized after he got booted from the Bureau.

Minimalism had been his thing since then, in spite of being employed again and getting a raise.

He didn't need things in his life.

Greyson studied the two women.

"I'm in no hurry," he told Rachel.

She was off like a shot into the back of the shop, back to where Liz kept the Romance books, entire walls of those books there, organized alphabetically by sub-genre rather than author. Said it paid off most of her bills every month, just turning that stock over to office drones in the nearby towers looking for a better escape than drudgery and retirement.

"So I know you haven't retired yet, like you threatened to again," Liz began leadingly.

"Got a good enough offer from the Metropolitan to stay on for a while," he replied. "Training the kid for the most part, until she's better than me. Dunno after that."

"You could do London when she goes," Liz offered, reminding Greyson that the two women had bonded over books since last fall.

That they had an entire cop/informant relationship he didn't know about. Didn't want to know about. Didn't care.

Why Rachel was reading Cop/Alien erotica in her spare time was not a topic he felt like pursuing, either. As long as everyone involved were portrayed as consenting adults, whatever kinks anyone wanted to work out on paper weren't his problem.

Rachel emerged a few seconds later with a pair of oversized paperback books in hand. She set them down on the counter and Greyson confirmed that the lurid, purple spines had *20* and *21* at the bottom.

He had his classical music and his synth whiskey, who was he to judge?

Rachel peeled put a sammie, a twenty dollar coin with a

salmon on the front, and set it on top of the pile, almost vibrating with excitement.

Greyson made sure he didn't pull something, rolling his eyes too hard at the woman.

Women.

Liz bagged the books and made change before turning her attention back his way.

"So what else brings you two lovely citizens to my den?" she asked in an innocent way.

"Need some words," Greyson replied.

Liz laughed before she could catch herself, and chortled as she gestured to the floor-to-ceiling racks of new and used books around them.

Greyson let himself grin. He actually liked Liz, unlike a lot of the folks he had to talk to.

"Which words?" she finally managed, still sputtering a little.

"There was a shooting downtown a few days ago," he said. "Man with a gun firing bullets."

"I heard about that," Liz replied, her voice dropping a little.

"I was the one who took the shooter down," Greyson confirmed the unspoken question in her eyes. "He had a Synth Chip socketed behind his ear."

"While he was shooting?" she asked sharply. "How is that possible?"

"Same thing I want to know," Greyson said. "Hoping you might know a few people in one of those shadier corners you could introduce me to. Not after them, and don't give a damn about whatever kinks they hack chips to run. Not today, probably not tomorrow. Right up there with Cop/Alien porn erotica novels. But this chip came from off-planet."

"An alien chip for humans?" she gasped. "Why?"

"This one also didn't have cutouts in it," Greyson continued. "According to the initial report from the lab, that apparently was by design, and not accidental. Plus he had a gun, an old Ruger revolver. Something bad is going on and I need to step past a lot of little things to find the big one."

He pulled a twenty out as well and slipped it over the counter and onto her keyboard, out of sight of anyone happening to wander in, although Liz had cameras everywhere and wouldn't be surprised.

She still had a cover to maintain.

Her face grew closed in concentration.

"Let me make a few calls," she said. "I know a few folks, tangential connections in the entertainment services industry, but they might not want to talk to cops."

"Understood," he replied. "Mostly just looking for background here. Underground circuit of things, because nobody local was involved. Not even as a dupe, because too many things came together for anything less than a conspiracy. Plus, other cops might want to rattle their cages and I'm pretty sure that none of your friends have done anything I care about."

"Noted," she said, smiling, but it was fake. Grim. "I'll let you know tonight or tomorrow, depending when they get back to me."

"Thanks, Liz," he nodded.

Rachel had watched silently, but immediately headed for the exit with him, her two new books in a little bag.

"Now what?" she asked as they got back out into the sunlight and crossed the street onto the Common.

He walked all the way out to where Carl was serving bad coffee and pastries maybe a day or two past fresh without speaking. She kept up, but Rachel also knew his patterns.

He got a small coffee and avoided the rest. Carl smiled as he made change.

Greyson picked a direction at random and walked. Rachel had skipped the nasty sludge Carl brewed, but she also knew better. Greyson wasn't going to have more than a sip or two before trashing it.

Nobody turned suddenly as he shifted directions randomly. Maybe that meant nothing. Maybe they already had a sniffer hidden on his Bureau-issued Skycruiser and could just wait for him to drive off.

"Now, I think I want the afternoon off," he said finally. "You go do some homework so you can read your new books as a prize later."

"Gonna call Emmy?" she grinned.

"Maybe," Greyson replied. "She's a busy woman, so things are usually on her schedule, not mine."

"Yeah, but if you suddenly had an afternoon free and needed to let cop-brain ruminate, I'm pretty sure she'd move meetings around so you two could go to a movie and dinner. And whatever."

Greyson shrugged. Rachel Asher had a pretty good understanding of how he worked by now. But Greyson wasn't all that complicated as a man. At least he didn't think so.

Simple needs. Simple life. Hell, simple apartment with most of his old books sold off to collectors by Liz when he downsized and reevaluated everything.

The question he needed to answer was how much longer he wanted to be a cop. A Hunter. Especially if folks were building up the sorts of elaborate conspiracies that he and Rachel had suggested, with him, Parsons, and maybe Denise as targets.

Not many people out there hated all three of them equally. He could think of a few.

One, in particular, but Greyson Leigh wasn't sure he was angry enough to go do something to the man.

Not yet, anyway.

[5]
KNOCK KNOCK

GREYSON WALKED TO THE DOOR AND PEEKED THROUGH the eyehole, just to be sure. His jacket was hanging over the one chair, leaving him with the shoulder holster for the nerve scrambler visible and the palmstunner tucked into his belt.

He'd offered her her own key to the door, as often as she came over to spend the evening or the night, but Emmy refused.

Said it was his space and he needed to reserve it for just himself.

Greyson wasn't sure he understood her logic, but he barely understood the woman and what she saw in him. Still, he undid the locks and opened the door.

Emelina Aitana Antúnez.

Tall and dusky. Mexican, originally, before the aliens made national borders a quaint thing, but pureblood Spanish even then going back centuries.

Brown hair bobbed just long enough to grab hold of in one hand and pull in certain circumstances. Dark eyes that didn't miss anything. Body that just didn't stop.

He had at least a decade on the woman, but she could

run men fresh out of boot camp into the ground if she wanted. Had, before he stumbled across her as part of an investigation and apparently caught her eye.

She had a look like a hunter spying a sprung trap as she crossed the threshold.

"I told Danzer he could handle everything for the rest of the day," she said conversationally, stepping close and kissing him without making any other physical contact. "No big deals or contracts that needed to be handled until tomorrow at the earliest."

Greyson had met Emmy's attorney a few times. If he hadn't already know her, he might have thought the man was a dangerous predator. A shark in shallow waters.

Danzer was really a remora compared to her.

He returned the kiss, flipping the door shut as he did.

Eventually, he leaned back from kissing the woman and took her in.

Yeah.

Five feet, nine inches of dancer. The kind that saw the Argentinian Tango as a warm-up for serious dancing. At least he could lead.

"So I'm not interrupting any major corporate takeovers?" Greyson asked.

All that, and she was a shark. Fabulously wealthy businesswoman on her ninth start-up, if he had the math right. Four had gone public or been bought outright by major industrial players. Her personal wealth was right at the bottom of the top thousand of humans alive after her last venture had worked out. He didn't even know what she actually did, except that Emmy found companies other people missed, usually start-ups needing a shot of something.

She bought them, or bought in. Found them that missing piece. Turned around and sold her stake six or twelve months later, sometimes making back something like one hundred times her original investment.

On the streets, he would have called her a fixer. Maybe they also did up in the corporate towers where Emmy ruled.

She stepped past him with a chuckle and Greyson watched her walk. There wasn't enough light, but it didn't look like she was wearing anything under that royal blue, A-line sun dress.

"There are a few out there," she smiled, turning slowly back to show him her profile, backlit by the kitchenette. "Wounded rabbit sort of thing. Danzer can run them down for now."

"That's good," Greyson joined her grin, stepping around the luscious woman to the counter, where there was already a pair of glasses next to the synth whiskey bottle.

He poured as she stepped right up and pressed herself against his back, laying her cheek on his shoulder and wrapping her hands around his stomach.

"You're more fun when you're a cop," she sighed. "Greyson Leigh was amazing without that badge, but it does something to you. Something arousing."

He nodded carefully.

He was Greyson Leigh. She had not been able to tell otherwise.

Greyson did laundry religiously, so that the smell of a Phrenic body was never obvious.

Ethen Boli had killed Greyson last fall. Taken his form and his mind. Maybe his soul.

A Phrenic used a projection of their victim to imitate them. Like hiding behind a living screen of Greyson Leigh so he could get inside the coming investigation after Ethen had killed Dominguez but been interrupted in his feeding by Rachel Asher.

Greyson had been too much to handle. Or maybe the

cop had offered Ethen a way out of being a serial killer and a fool.

Still waters ran deep.

Ethen's partner Zaborra had shot him—them—there at the end. Killed him. Killed them.

Should have turned Ethen Boli into a Deathwalker.

Except that Greyson Leigh had turned around inside their head and looked right at him. Offered to save them both, if Ethen would just let go and let him handle things.

He was Greyson today. Ethen had retreated and hid, except when Greyson needed to ask him a question.

Neither of them were certain what a medical scanner would show, but weren't about to risk finding out.

Rachel had her suspicions. Greyson was pretty sure on that score.

Emmy just thought he had been reborn.

Maybe Greyson had, in a way. Surviving certain death was likely to do that to a middle-aged cop with nothing to lose except this amazing woman leaning her weight on him.

Except that Emmy weighed nothing at all. Just thinking about her held him up like a helium balloon some days.

He turned inside her arms with a glass in each hand. Kissed her again because she was warm, and welcoming, and smiled at him.

"Wanna go see a movie?" he asked innocently.

She shifted her weight to stand up, snagging the highball glass from his hand with a sly grin. She took a sip.

"Can we sit in the back row and make out like teenagers?" she asked.

"Sure," Greyson grinned back. "Except that you're dressed all wrong for me to try to slip a hand up your shirt and feel your breasts."

"The cotton's almost as good as bare skin," she purred. "Maybe better for a little roughness in the right places. And if you put your jacket over me, I might just slip the shoulder straps off."

He took a drink with a laugh and then kissed her, relishing the taste of whiskey on his tongue and smell of the flowers on her skin.

"Surprised you wanted to go anywhere," she said in an offhand way.

"Gotta keep you on your toes," Greyson smiled. "Don't want to get all stodgy and predictable. You might decide to trade me on a younger model."

"You find me anyone as good as you and I might, but you're pretty safe."

"I'll keep you away from Rachel, then," Greyson shrugged, slipping loose and dragging her to the couch so they could settle and he could watch Emmy fold her long, brown legs under her like a cat.

"Your partner like girls?" Emmy asked in a voice that even sounded innocent.

"I haven't inquired," he said simply. "Enough people think we're fooling around that they make mistakes underestimating me. Us."

"And you're not?" she asked. It was an innocent question, rather than a jealous one.

He had no claim on her, beyond what time she could carve out from corporate takeovers and board meetings. He was a cop who kept bizarre hours.

"Too many cops end up fooling around when they have a pretty woman as a partner," Greyson replied. "Human nature, as that might be the only person that they see who understands the job. The stress. I was never home enough to be married when I was in the army or later. I keep Rachel at arm's length. Not my type."

"Really?" Emmy asked. "What's not to like? Maybe she's a little short, but she's got better muscles than even I do.

Smart as a whip. Lethal, too. Even a similar skin color and hair. Maybe her family are three generations removed from Puerto Rico, but still."

"I need to keep my life in compartments," he said, turning so she could see the truth in his eyes. "Cop things. Music things. Personal things."

"And I'm a personal thing?" she asked with a lascivious grin on her bright red lips.

"About as personal as it gets, Emmy," he replied. "You remind me what it's like to be human, when I get too deep into the Bureau. You pull me back when I start to drift out to sea."

He paused to take a drink of the whiskey, wondering why he was baring his soul to this woman today. Except that it was Emmy. She knew most of what there was to know about Greyson Leigh.

Nothing of Ethen Boli, but that was for the best.

"I'm on a new case," he admitted when she just sat and sipped, watching him like a predator.

"The shooting?" she asked, showing that she'd been following the news. And had her own channels for information, since his name hadn't been attached to it and he hadn't seen her in a week.

"It was a setup," Greyson nodded. "Perp with an illegal firearm. Alien Synth Chip that had been hacked to override its programming and the human wearing it. And my picture in his pocket."

"Oh, shit," she gasped, suddenly, finally looking less like a corporate titan and more like a concerned woman.

That was why he could carve out time for Emmy. She could make that transition. Not many people could.

Greyson took another sip and nodded.

"Rachel thinks that whoever it is has set something in motion to take down me, Parsons, and even Upkins."

"You going to Florida to rattle some cages?" she asked after a moment.

"The thought had crossed my mind," he said ominously. "Zielinski certainly fits that order of lading. And has enough of an ax to grind. Not sure yet, as I only got dragged into this case a few hours ago. Putting some irons into the fire, but they need time to get hot. Decided to take the afternoon off and see if you wanted a play date."

"Absolutely," she smiled warmly. "And maybe after the movie you can stick your iron in my fire."

He chuckled and finished off his glass. She did the same, and unfolded in such a way that she ended up draped across him.

Emmy put both glasses on the floor and was suddenly in his lap like the cat he'd never owned.

"Lemme guess," she said in between kisses. "You need the movie to let your brain settle into digesting information. And then you're expecting me to take you off-line later, followed by dinner?"

"Hoping," he countered. "Never expecting. Not with you. Hoping."

She smiled and kissed him full. Greyson thought he could feel the purrs in her chest where he held her.

Before they got too involved, he stood up, lifting her weight as well as his and letting her hang there for a moment before she dropped lithely to the floor.

She broke from him and walked towards the door. She paused at the chair and grabbed his jacket, putting it around her shoulders for a moment like an opera cape with a twirl before handing it to him.

"We'll need this," she said, looking somehow like a precocious seventeen-year-old for a moment.

Greyson could barely remember being that old, but that had been nearly thirty years ago now.

He slipped his jacket on and figured that it would all come back pretty quickly.

He needed to think. Then she was right. He'd need to go off-line.

Tomorrow, he was going to start hunting.

[6]

MORNING

GREYSON STRETCHED AND SIPPED SOME MORE COFFEE.

Emmy being Emmy, she'd been up an hour before dawn checking the markets and then out the door with a kiss before he rolled back over and slept until the sun coming through the curtains woke him again. After that, first coffee and an hour at his fold-down table reading whatever he could about the perp and the case file.

At least as he was getting older, he was keeping in better shape. Otherwise, Greyson was pretty sure a woman like Emmy might just fuck him to death. Not that it would be a bad way to go, but still.

Late morning now. Lots of snide commentary from Rachel over brunch, but at least they'd found a spot indoors, so he didn't have to listen for gunshots. Northside joint that was open twenty-four hours, transitioning from night owls to office drones without missing a beat. Dive instead of café, just to get away from everyone as the sun outside threatened to be spring if he didn't pay attention.

Rachel was just teasing, though. He'd warned her that he was sleeping in this morning, so she'd done the same and was attacking a late breakfast right now while they discussed details of the new case.

Greyson didn't really bother with the man's name, except as a placeholder. It was obviously a setup of some sort, and Metro PD was handling the local aspects.

Eventually, he was sure they'd all run into solid dead ends that would bring their case to a grinding halt. The revolver would end up being a custom print job out of some black fab that didn't believe in maker's marks. Ditto the ammunition.

The man had turned out to be a mid-level corporate manager type. Divorced and paying alimony. Couple of teenage kids he probably saw on every other weekend.

Some things never change.

Greyson's grandmother had had the right idea, fifty years ago. A couple wanting to get married should be required to live with each other for at least two years before they could get married and be allowed to turn off the birth control meds. Then they could have a family.

But only after they had determined that it was a good idea. Too many of the folks he'd gone to high school with had married someone within a year of graduating. Usually a kid either on the way or right after that. Then too many of them divorced within five years.

Or: Why Greyson Leigh had never bothered…

No, the shooter himself would be another dead end. Whoever had set him up would have had to make a couple of really egregious mistakes to be tracked, and the rest of this didn't feel like amateur hour.

Only the Synth Chip stood out.

Alien design. Maybe made in an alien fabrication plant, but if you had the designs right, then almost any competent body shop could probably turn it out, from what he'd seen in other cases.

Greyson was still waiting for Forensics to call in some

favors with the Illymus Merchant Guild to see which of the various alien species out there might have done the work.

Greyson had never been farther off-planet than one of the orbital resorts. He knew there were hundreds of inhabited planets out there, but he was a human cop. Close enough, anyway.

Ethen had been any number of interesting places, but he hated remembering them because of all the people he'd killed, either to rob, rape, or because he needed an escape from cops like Greyson Leigh closing in on him.

Rachel was studying him now as he circled 'round the case in his head, like a shark sniffing for blood.

He just looked a whole battery of questions at her.

She glanced around, but the dive they were in was mostly empty, in that mid-morning stretch where folks go elsewhere for a coffee break, and haven't reached even an early lunch.

He glanced at his comm. 10:13. Weird time of day to be just getting into motion.

"I don't know how to ask this," she finally admitted.

"Not like you're going to offend me, most likely," he countered.

"True," Rachel agreed. "So I'll just kind of drop a turd in the punch bowl and then we can figure it out. Okay?"

He scowled at the young woman and drank some more coffee.

"If we need to go off-world to investigate this, is it safe for you?" she asked in a voice so quiet he was pretty much reading her lips.

Greyson felt the cold hand of Death herself reach out and grab him lightly by the scruff of the neck before giving him a quick squeeze.

Rachel saw it, too, but didn't move, except that the light in her eyes changed.

He could deny everything, but that would be *pro forma*.

She'd just gotten the answer she needed. All the truth there was.

Greyson wondered if she was about to shoot him with her nerve scrambler. It would be over fast at this range, since he wouldn't bother dodging.

He'd be dead. Then Ethen would have maybe a split second to decide if he wanted to join him.

Then there would be a dead Phrenic body laying on the floor, dressed in Greyson's clothes.

Or maybe there was a sniper nearby? Except that they'd need to be in the restaurant.

Nobody in here gave off cop vibes, even to Greyson's sense of smell.

He just stared at her for a long moment, wondering if it was all over now.

Rachel didn't move. Just breathed, slow and regular.

"I don't like off-world travel," Greyson finally said in a carefully-neutral tone. "If it came to that, I'd probably just send you to dig after any leads that came up. You're almost as good at this game as I am."

Almost? Yeah, maybe he still had a few tricks to teach Patrolman/Hunter Rachel Lupita Asher, if it came down to that.

She nodded and picked up her coffee. Greyson remembered to breathe.

"I could do that for you," she said evenly, having gotten the answer she was looking for.

Greyson Leigh wasn't really human. Or rather, Greyson Leigh's soul had taken possession of the Phrenic impostor who had originally killed him, and now he was the Deathwalker playing at being a Detective/Hunter.

Or something.

Nobody could tell, because Ethen had let go. Had let Greyson have their body. As long as he did his sheets and laundry every three or four days, and showered daily, the sharp, ammonia smell of a Phrenic wouldn't ever build up enough that someone could pick it up.

Not even a dog, unless they were specifically trained for that sort of thing. And only then after they'd held him in a cell for a few days.

Greyson would burn that bridge when he got there. He and Ethen were already living on borrowed time.

"Besides, you're the one that wants to join Scotland Yard," Greyson reminded her. "I'm just the last trainer you have in Boston before you get your degree."

He could tell she wanted to deflect the whole conversation with some off-hand joke, but she refrained. Just stared at him for a long moment.

"Is there anybody better at this job than you?" she finally asked.

"No," Greyson replied after a moment of reflection. "You will be eventually, if you keep at it for another few years and get your degree. And learn everything I can teach you in the meantime. But I'm the best. Not even the dead guys you might mention come close. They were always junior varsity when I was around."

"And now?" she pursued.

"Hunter Bureau loses one hell of a cop when you take the lateral," Greyson said. "I'll probably just retire again at that point, unless you need me over there for something."

"Would you come?" She seemed surprised.

"If you were the one asking?" he fired back.

She nodded.

"Probably," Greyson concluded. "Nothing ties me to Boston."

"Not even Upkins?" Her eyes got mischievous.

"Denise and I were a thing a long time ago," Greyson said. "Before she got serious about becoming Metropolitan. I

43

had too many secrets then to be safe for her. Got more now."

"Ain't that the truth," Rachel said, but she left it off there.

Didn't follow up with the obvious secret. The six hundred pound gorilla she'd brought up.

The fact that an alien ship or station would subject him to a routine scan when he came aboard. And they would be programmed to look for Phrenic infiltrators.

The species was fine as long as they followed the rules and subjected themselves to everyone else's paranoia. It was the rogues that made a lot of those scanners necessary. And the collar that would keep a base-form Phrenic from shapeshifting so you knew what you were dealing with and didn't have to fear them.

When you could kill someone and steal all their memories, and even their DNA, you could go anywhere. Do anything.

Even inspire humans to create the Hunter Bureau, when they needed to stop such killers.

Greyson didn't know what such a scan might show. Nobody would, unless he and Rachel decided to break into a black ops body shop and use their scanner.

Sure, it was his DNA. His memories. His soul.

Was it in his body? Or Ethen's?

Greyson finally decided that she wasn't about to take him down, so he gestured the girl with the pot for a refill of his mug.

He was going to burn a lot of calories, if he was about to dig hard into the soft underbelly of Boston's crime scene for an alien contact that didn't want a Hunter coming.

But that was a decision the fool should have made a month ago, when he could still survive what was coming.

Greyson was pissed and looking for someone to take it out on.

[7]

FASHION

Rachel wasn't sure what Greyson's game was as he drove the big cruiser downtown. The man was counting streets and buildings in his head, obviously, but not even muttering right now.

Silence, but for the sound of the wheels on the street outside the car. She'd pushed just about as hard as she felt was safe earlier, but he'd handled it with all his usual gruff aplomb and overall *fuck you*.

But he had confirmed it for her. Enough, anyway.

She'd had nightmares after that night. Seeing Greyson Leigh suddenly turn into a base model Phrenic before her eyes, before turning back into himself and chasing down their serial killer.

She'd been concussed pretty hard when he threw her out of the way of an incoming bolt, but not so hard that she didn't trust her eyes. Or her memory.

She'd wondered that night, with a dead Phrenic lying next to a live Leigh, but what if there had been two of them? If the one that had killed Dominguez and failed when she showed up, if that one had gone on and gotten Greyson Leigh before he knew that he was back in the great game?

But he'd just sat there waiting for her to shoot him, like he didn't care.

Maybe he didn't. Or maybe the Phrenic was in hell now and Greyson was in charge.

She'd never heard of anything like that, but she'd also never met anybody, of any species, as stubborn as that man.

And this morning he'd frozen up when she'd asked. Pretty much as big an admission of guilt as you could get without actually speaking.

And Rachel Asher hadn't shot him.

Should she? Everything he'd said and done for the last six months had been pretty much dedicated to making her a better cop. A better Hunter.

It was like the Phrenic was gone and there was just Greyson. Or maybe this was what pure atonement looked like, where the thing using Leigh's memories was trying to make up for a life of crime and stupid decisions.

If the truth ever came out, her name would be mud for not seeing it, so she supposed that there was a little bit of self-preservation there, too, but even Emmy hadn't stopped her relationship, and she was much closer to the man.

Rachel shook her head as they pulled into an underground parking garage and started spiraling down to the very bottom. The depths of Boston, as it were.

Greyson always drove like a race car driver, with a sureness of motion she'd never gotten right. It was like the man had been born to drive.

Most cars these days were autonomous by default, but he always disabled those circuits as soon as the car started.

Staying in control at all times.

Another lesson for her, Rachel was pretty sure.

Don't let others think or act for you until you have no choice in the matter.

Damn it, Greyson Leigh was going to be a pain in the ass, trying to live up to that kind of legend.

Bottom floor of the garage wasn't as full as the uppers. But this section of Boston wasn't honeycombed with tunnels yet. Give it another generation and the alien digging machines would have created a whole second world down here where nobody ever had to see the sun again.

As opposed to those few who did that now.

Leigh pulled them into an empty spot and shut the car down.

"You ready for this?" he asked, but it was mostly perfunctory.

She nodded and they exited the vehicle.

Liz's instructions had been precise, and bizarre. They started right back up the ramp they'd just driven down, but on foot this time.

Walking.

One in four of the lights on these two levels were burned out, in spite of the aliens selling them tech that was better than that. Maybe it hadn't made it this far yet.

Or maybe it was on purpose.

Rachel felt like they should have been dressed snazzier, at least for going into the underground itself, metaphorically as well as physically.

In the old vids from before she was born, the dark future had always been full of rain or at least drizzle. Something to convey an overall grayness and depression.

Characters wore protective gear, because the rain that fell was largely poisonous and acidic in all those stories, too. Greyson would be in a brown longcoat right now, since he was the hero. Collar up and maybe with one of those weird belts on it that folks did. The ones that they tied instead of buckling, which made no damned sense.

Hats had gone out in the 1960s. US President Kennedy had managed to kill an entire industry, all by himself, just by deciding not to wear one but she could see Leigh in an old fedora or something similar.

She would be the gruff dame, but a pencil skirt wasn't something she ever planned to own, unless it was for a party where they had to dress uncomfortably. Heels? Gimme a break.

And they hadn't done androgynous in those days. Being less than stridently hetero in the late 20th Century was an invitation to get beat up.

Fucking barbarians.

Still, Rachel figured she'd be in baggy slacks, maybe with those weird, two-toned shoes. Zoot suit, maybe? Just to completely mess with people.

"Why are you snickering?" Greyson muttered quietly as they emerged up onto the flat part of the second level and started across the lot.

She glanced over at the man as they moved. He wore those combat boots she'd liked so much that she owned two pairs now, black like his and her current ones in dark brown.

Tough slacks for the bit of chill Boston still got, but nothing like heavy wool they might have done a century ago. White shirts, crisp and buttoned. Matching jacket.

He had two buttons on his and she was stylisher with three, but again.

"We'll need to up our fashion game at some point," Rachel replied.

She could pretty much smell the sarcastic eyeroll that ensued, and grinned.

"Kid, I burned all my ties," Greyson muttered back. "Not buying new ones."

"Oh, Greyson, this will go so much beyond new ties," she giggled quietly. "Might have to rope Emmy into it."

"That's what frightens me, Rachel," he grumbled.

They continued across, turning down a little side corridor that was almost completely hidden behind some pillars. Rachel assumed it was a place for maintenance and service folks, away from the natural flow of foot traffic into the lifts and stairs.

Didn't want the beautiful people subjected to the ugly spaces.

Just mutts like me.

She was a stride back and on Greyson's right. He was right-handed to her left, so it put shooting hands on the inside, if someone jumped out at them.

Always plan for violence. Another Greyson Leigh public service announcement.

The corridor was bleak. She couldn't find a better word to describe it. Dingy with streaks of spilled *something* on the floor. The lights were almost yellow with age, instead of the pure white of the newer tech. She wondered if they were actual fluorescent bulbs, rather than LED or something exotic.

How wild, to find something that old.

Service elevator. Again, battered and scratched, like someone, or a whole bunch of someones had stood here and rammed the stainless steel door too many times with carts and such.

Rachel calmed herself and took a deep sniff, just to fix the place in her memory.

Industrial kind of smell. The oil from the floor. Rust. Unwashed bodies, but not that recently.

Ozone.

Really? Ozone?

Greyson pushed the call button and they waited. The door opened quickly enough and they stepped in.

This was where Liz's instructions got hinky.

Greyson waited for the doors to close, and then pressed the emergency contact button. The red one down in the corner.

"Leigh and Asher," he said conversationally. "We have an appointment."

She stood and waited, wondering at all the cloak and dagger stuff. But she supposed that these folks were career criminals who might not appreciate cops nosing around.

Even Hunters like her.

The lift started moving again, but down, not up.

Right back down to the bottom-most level.

Weirdly, there were two sets of doors in here. She'd noticed it, but not connected the dots.

The back one opened now.

She and Greyson turned.

An even darker, dingier corridor stretching away.

She wondered if someone had blocked up the elevator door behind her. The one back out into the real world, and not whatever Alice in Wonderland realm she had just entered.

Greyson started to walk, so she followed, still back and to his right.

The ozone smell was sharper here, but the smell of bodies less. Maybe a little incense, or a higher quality patchouli going.

Felt like a steam tunnel. The sort of place where she and Greyson had killed that other Phrenic.

How much of the terrain under-Boston was riddled with ancient tunnels like this that people had eventually forgotten about?

There was a door down at the end of the corridor.

Double, but metal. Big camera over the center, rather than the pinhole type that had probably been watching them for however long.

She wondered if they trusted AIs with their security down here. Made a certain bit of sense, just because they were supposed to be electronic gearheads, but you had to program those things well to deal with all the sensory input.

Too much risk of overload.

Greyson reached into his inner jacket pocket and pulled out his badge and ID. She did the same.

They held them up to the camera and let the machine take its own long sniff.

Cop-smell, but more importantly, Hunter-smell.

You boys don't have anything to fear from us, unless one of you is an illegal alien serial killer. Then maybe the gloves have to come off.

Rachel wondered if she could give off that kind of scent in a way that a camera could pick it up.

Worth trying.

She finally understood how serious these folks were when she heard four big bolts retract in the door. Two up. Two down. Probably stop anything short of military ordnance. At least give the folks on the other side a lot of lead time to get the hell out of Dodge.

The door lock buzzed and Greyson pressed it in.

The backside of that beast was a little nicer. Carpet now, on the floor and walls, even if it was mismatched. Like someone on one of the upper floors had redecorated and the scraps ended up down here instead of a recycling plant.

Not the whole rainbow, but certainly the spectrum of colors Rachel liked to think of as *Corporate*. All the soft browns and greens, with some blues and quieter reds thrown in.

It was another room, but this one had three doors leading

off into wherever. Interior doors, but Rachel was willing to bet that those were just shells over old bank vaults someone had found in a dump or something.

The place had that sort of a feel to it.

"Scanner says you're both armed," a man's voice came out of a speaker. "You'll have to leave them here."

"No," Greyson spoke up suddenly. "I don't think so."

[8]
CHIPTECH

GREYSON HAD BEEN EXPECTING SOME SORT OF POWER play. Kid's games in a sandbox.

Bullies were usually just the ones who'd been picked on as kids and wanted to return the favor. Mad at the world. Greyson had gotten most of that beaten out of him in the Army.

Most.

The bits that were left were generally the ones the Army had found useful as tools. Deliberate cruelty. Premeditated self-defense.

He waited, feeling Rachel bristle a little next to him.

She didn't have enough years on this stupid planet to handle punks like this the right way.

But gumbo is just ingredients for the first hour or so. The magic only happens later.

He figured he'd given them enough time to sweat.

"We're Hunters, not cops," he said, as if the guy was standing right here. "I'm looking for background information on someone who's trying to make you folks look bad. Liz steered me this way, because she likes you and she trusts us."

Greyson let that hang in the air like a ripe fart for a few moments.

"If that won't work, let me know and we'll head right back out," he continued. "Your secrets will be safe with us, and I'll find someone else to help me hunt alien assassins."

There. Remind them that Hunters are after more interesting, more dangerous, game.

He felt like smiling, but worried that his face might break if he did. It had been that kind of a day.

Week.

Whatever it was.

Longer pause this time, like maybe someone had muted the line at his end and was arguing with someone else.

Greyson had never had a reason to engage with underground chip fabrication plants, so he had no idea how they worked. Or how big they might be.

The Merchant's Guild, those aliens that had catapulted humanity into the galactic age, embargoed certain tech as too destabilizing for the silly monkeys on Earth, but Greyson figured that there were always going to be smugglers out there, up to no good.

Money talks and bullshit walks, as his grandfather would have said right now. Greyson missed the old man some days.

"I've got a personal security system inside here," the man's voice came back now. "If you make any sudden or rash moves it is likely to start shooting, so consider yourself on notice."

Greyson nodded. About what he'd expected. Not like these were law-abiding people down here. They would need automated defense turrets to keep outsiders honest.

The door on his right buzzed and Greyson moved to it. He pulled it open on the second try after pushing first and found himself in a white tiled corridor that reminded him of an old hospital. Or maybe what this place had been when it was first laid down as another underground tunnel connecting buildings. Back when winters had been so bad that the cost to dig was better than having people have to gear up to cross quads.

He entered this new world, wondering if the door straight ahead had been a trap, or maybe just a fake added over a concrete wall to make real cops spend a lot of time blowing it open and giving people more time to flee.

This whole place felt like a complex puzzle, but he was a Hunter because that sort of thing appealed to him.

He noted the turret in the ceiling as it tracked them with a camera and a stunner, walking down the tunnel.

Greyson hoped it was a stunner.

There were doors down this hallway. One on the right was open and had a light on, so he set off in that direction.

The space reminded him of a mad hacker lab from some vid. He wondered how much of the fiction was true and how much was something the people in the industry adopted.

His favorite hacker had been having drinks with him one night when her comm beeped. When asked, she had told Greyson that she had just managed to access the old Federal Reserve system. While having a glass of wine and dressed up snazzy enough that he always felt a little grubby next to her.

Greyson wondered if Melanie had finally retired, or just been forced to disappear on the run when the authorities who cared about those sorts of things got too close.

The man behind the desk stood up and held out a hand as Greyson entered the large office.

He was giant. Tall, tough-looking black guy. Greyson wasn't sure what the accepted denomination was these days. It had been *Negro* once, then *Black*, then *African-American*.

In a galaxy with that many alien species running around, *Human* had become the way Greyson categorized everyone.

The stranger's hair was shaved tight on the sides and faded up into a mohawk that had been picked straight at some point. About three inches tall and damned impressive.

Greyson took the hand and waited for the man to squeeze. He had to be at least six foot ten, and built pretty normal, when most of them tended to be beanpoles.

He did the obvious and went for the crush. A punk-ass bully.

Greyson smiled after a moment and returned the favor. Ethen's bones were more flexible than a human's, underneath it all. Even if the DNA was Greyson Leigh.

Tall Guy's eyes popped a little. Greyson stopped short of doing permanent damage. The man needed his hands for his keyboards.

"Hell of a grip you got there," the man said as he got his hand back.

"Sometimes aliens don't want to come willingly," Greyson offered as a distraction, not mentioning that those generally just got shot and dragged home.

"Quinton Laux," the tall man introduced himself, gesturing to a pair of chairs on Greyson's side of the messy desk with at least three monitors facing inward to Laux.

"Greyson Leigh," he said, taking an old chair that looked like someone had stolen it from a dentist's front office.

You know the kind: square tubes bent into legs and back, with enough padding to be called that, but not enough to be comfortable. The cloth was an ugly mustard these days, but it probably hadn't faded too much. Greyson remembered one from when he was a kid.

"Rachel Asher," she growled, not offering to play games with the guy.

That tall, she'd probably go after one of his knees if she

got angry enough. They were high enough to reach easily. And Rachel was that mean.

He noted another turret overhead. Probably fast enough to get both of them if they got stupid. Laux had nothing to fear.

At least so far.

"Liz told me about you," the man began, sounding like an insurance salesman all of a sudden. "What brings you thus, Detective/Hunter Leigh?"

"There was a mass shooting on the surface a week ago," Greyson replied simply.

"Heard about that," the man offered vaguely.

"The shooter had a Synth Chip in his data-jack when he went down," Greyson continued, watching Laux's face for emotions.

He got most of them. Surprise, concern, fear, anger, even maybe a little joy. Hard to tell.

"You can't do that," he said after a moment in a shocked awe. "But I suppose that's why you wanted to talk to me, isn't it?"

"Partly," Greyson agreed. "The design is not human, according to my forensics folks, but they've never seen anything like it, either. According to them, any competent fab could turn the product out, though."

That last bit was a lie, but only a little one. They hadn't had time to tell, but he didn't have to give Laux anything to work with.

Laux started typing, but it was on his side of the desk. Screens faced away. Greyson waited. He was in no particular hurry, especially if Liz thought that this man was good enough to answer some of Greyson's questions.

Might make a useful contact for the two of them later.

"So I see him shooting," Laux said. "Old revolver like a cowboy vid. No useful security cameras in the area saw him put the chip in, so we presume he did that at home or something?"

Greyson wondered what camera feeds the man had tapped or if he had recorded it off some network when it happened.

Who knew how these folks worked or thought?

"Oh, that's interesting," Laux said suddenly, looking up now. Studying both of them like maybe he just realized that Rachel was a woman, and not just Greyson's vindictive shadow. "You took him down. Both of you."

Might be a little respect and maybe some awe in that voice now. Hard to tell. Certainly a breakthrough emotionally.

Greyson turned to Rachel to continue the story. Might be worth seeing how the man reacted to a really pretty woman he knew had a nerve scrambler nestled next to her breast.

"He was in the middle of a scenario called *Killer*, according to what we know right now," she took up the thread. "You get to play a madman with a gun, randomly walking into a crowd and shooting people."

Greyson watched Laux's eyes get a little bigger, but couldn't tell if the man was accessing something via a data-jack. He presumed it, since being able to get data straight to your brain would give anyone one hell of an edge against mere humans.

AIs were still going to think faster, but they had to be programmed to handle all the craziness a human could come up with, so organics still had an edge there.

"Any chance I could look at the encoding on the chip?" the man asked, suddenly a lot more friendly than he had been.

Greyson wondered how much of a technological revolution such a thing might be. Not for most tasks, but

Greyson could see the possibilities in a chip that completely overlaid your reality with tourist information in real time and let you still walk and talk instead of cutting you out for safety.

Datachips were just electronic guide books right now. You had to look something up and read about it, only in your head instead of your hands. If you wanted immersion, you had to wear a pair of goggles.

What if you could just socket a chip and everything around you *changed*?

Did the aliens have any idea what that might be worth to humans? It had only been sixteen years since they landed, after watching for a short time before that.

They might not yet fully *get* humans.

"Dunno on the Synth Chip," Greyson spoke up when Rachel looked over at him. "Not my case. I'm just trying to understand how they work, so I can figure out why someone did it. I want the who, not the how. But I'll ask."

"*How* a Synth Chip works is that it overrides all your sensory input channels," Laux said, leaning back and looking more like a middle-aged professor now than a punk.

Greyson upped his original estimation of the man's age to maybe thirty-five, wondering if he'd been forced underground or walked there himself.

This hidden vault would have still required money to pull off.

"That's all just electrical signals by the way, so it's not that hard to do, once you grow in all the neural circuitry around a data-jack," Laux continued lecturing. "Except that you need one of the newer, more expensive models to do full immersion. You think you are turning your head and the chip plays the scenery like you did. Think you're walking, and the system moves you in the fantasy."

"But you're cut out," Rachel pointed out. "Unable to actually interact."

"Correct," Laux nodded. "Because there is an artificial reality going on around you, you can walk into traffic without realizing it and get hit by a bus. Sounds like this one did a half-job, which is damned impressive code work. Keep most of reality, but probably filter it differently."

"Filter?" Greyson asked.

"Sure," Laux turned that smile his way. "Looks like they stopped being *people* and became *targets* to your shooter. He was interacting with a false reality that looked just like the normal one, and probably didn't know it. That's what a Synth Chip does. Gives you a fantasy so real you can't see the seams."

"How would you disable the cut-outs?" Greyson asked, waving away when the man started to object. "Yes, I know that's illegal, et cetera. Someone did it. I need to know how so I can go after the who."

"Because you already know the why?" he asked. "Liz said you were a pretty good cop, for not being one."

"I'm a Hunter, Laux," Greyson retorted. "The only time I get called in is to deal with aliens gone rogue."

"I can only guess about the overrides, Detective," Laux replied. "At least without studying the chip itself. All the sensory stuff coming in is normally just dumped. A legal Synth Chip has medical monitors and stuff so that it can turn itself off if something suddenly starts going wrong, but this thing sounds like it kept that data and did an overlay and didn't cut out all the voluntary muscles, which means it must have been beyond the cutting edge for chiptech. At least as humans know. Like you said, this is probably alien tech right now."

"Experimental?" Rachel spoke up now.

"And then some," Laux replied. "I'm pretty damned good

at coding those sorts of scenarios, but I'm not even sure how I'd go about rerouting everything. Unless—..."

"Unless?" Greyson asked after the men paused for too long, his eyes on some distant horizon.

"I was going to say unless he had a second chip somehow soldered onto the first internally," Laux said. "Put all the killer stuff on the outside one, but keep a medical-type monitor in place and route all your input through it. Wouldn't probably work in a fantasy setting, turning everyone into orcs or robots, but just adjusting your *Setting*, might be possible."

"Setting?"

"So in one of my other lives, I am also a writer," Laux puffed up a little with pride.

Must be pretty good. Greyson wondered what penname he wrote under, if Quinton Laux was a notorious hacker living in underBoston.

"Go on," Greyson prodded.

"A character exists in a setting," the man explained. "Not just a description of what you see, hear, and smell, but how you feel about it. How you interpret it."

"So if you see these people, you automatically hate them?" Rachel asked. "Smell their fear and that gives you *carte blanche* to just kill them, because they don't matter?"

"Something like that," Laux nodded. "I'd have your Forensics folks pop the case open if they haven't already and see if there are two, unrelated chips going on in there. The magic might be in the bridging software, rather than the Synth Chip itself."

He fell silent again. Thinking. Eyes flickering back and forth without focusing on anything in the room.

Finally, he returned to the present tense.

"In fact, I think I know how you might do it," he said. "At least knowing that it was done somehow. Wouldn't have thought of it on my own. Like you, I always thought that sort of thing was impossible."

Greyson reached into his pants pocket and pulled a stack of bills he kept there for those times when using a traceable credit system made contacts nervous.

He peeled a castor, a one hundred tooney note named for Castor the Beaver on the front, and set it on the desk, along with one of his business cards.

"I'd like to request that you maybe send me some of your thoughts, once you refine them, Laux," Greyson said. "And try not to flood the underground market with those chips, after you design them. At least not until you're sure they won't be turned to evil."

The man studied the bill, the card, and Greyson's face in equal amounts without speaking for a long moment.

"Information wants to be free, Leigh," he said simply. "Technology flows like water."

"Understood," Greyson agreed. "But I suspect that a new way of doing chips like that is a significant revolution. The next cyberpunk wave, if you will. You're likely to get rich on it, at least for a while. I'm hoping you can at least keep things on a more friendly keel, if only for a while."

"This is all just theoretical," Laux replied. "I'd have to actually study that chip to be sure. Any chance?"

"Not at the moment." Greyson decided to play the man honest. He'd done them good, just with the bits he'd been able to guess at.

Melanie had always maintained that a good code writer made so many personal decisions in the process that it was almost like leaving fingerprints behind. She'd frequently settled for second best or worse in code. What she called "script kiddie crap" because while she could write better stuff herself, it could subsequently be traced back to her, instead of some punk in Rome or Mexico City.

"Are you that good?" Greyson asked anyway.

He knew the answer he'd get, regardless of the actual truth. They all tended to be full of themselves.

"Maybe," Laux said, surprising Greyson. "But as you said, this might be a whole new way to handle architecture that nobody has ever thought of. A year from now some Vietnamese megafab will be churning them out for one of the big companies in entertainment by the pallet load, so I've probably got a month to solve the design and build it. Another month to write some scenarios, unless I hire some folks. Then the rest of that year to make some cash legitimately, before I have to go back to the underground kinks that you can't buy at the grocery store."

"Lemme talk to some people," Greyson offered, unsure who might be able to clear a career criminal to visit a police computer lab without being stripped naked first and sheep-dipped.

Good hackers never went into legitimate business for that long. The rules and dipshits they had to deal with weren't worth it. They could generally make much more money for way less hassle.

"Anything you can get me would shave days off the design," Laux said helpfully.

A hand dipped out of sight and came back with his business card.

Just the letter L and an email address that was entirely a random hash of numbers and letters, using the University of Prague's .edu ending.

Greyson didn't ask, just smiled and pocketed it as he rose.

"I'll send a ping to that address just so I don't have to type it more than once," Greyson acknowledged. "Then I'll ask. Anything you want to send to help me understand that design when I do have the schematics in front of me will help me convince them."

Laux rose and shook hands with both of them.

Greyson saw himself out, a silent Rachel in his shadowy wake. She waited until they were out in the parking garage to speak.

"People really live like that?" she asked in a voice filled with wonder and a little resentment.

"I doubt it," Greyson replied.

"How so, then?"

"The rest of that hallway goes somewhere," he pointed out. "Might emerge in some other residential tower where our friend lives. Or has an above-ground office. Pretty sure most of that was for show. Criminals like to look fancy and exotic, when most of them live in slums one step ahead of the men and women with badges. Computer crime is even harder, since everything you do has to pass through someone else's system, where it leaves traces and can be back-tracked."

"How do you know so much about white collar crime?" Rachel asked.

"Remind me to tell you about Melanie sometime," he grinned down at her. "Before Emmy. Like Laux, probably."

"He didn't impress me that much," she offered offhand.

"Then you weren't paying attention," Greyson said. "The ones that are that casual about it are usually the ones at the top of the game. Not the punks. He's probably already designing something in his head and will have a prototype ready by tomorrow, if I know the type."

"Then what?" Rachel asked.

"Not my problem, Rachel," he said. "Still chasing the asshole who gave our perp the chip, the gun, and my picture."

[9]

HUNTER

Greyson and Rachel had returned to the office after that. Hunters kept even weirder hours than police detectives, because frequently they were after people and creatures that only came out at night.

Occasionally, Greyson hoped for a case where the suspect got up a little after dawn and had a good breakfast in a nice restaurant, just so they could both get to bed at a reasonable hour.

This wasn't going to be that case, either.

He left Rachel upstairs filling out paperwork and doing her homework while he headed out the ground floor entrance on foot. Boston had enough of a decent public transit network that you could get anywhere with a little work. Or find a taxi reasonably cheap. Universal Basic Income kept people from starving, but they still needed something to do, so a lot of them took up driving strangers or doing hobbies that might make them some cash on the side.

Whatever floats your boat. It got him a few miles up the road, away from the office.

He needed time to process. Up until a few hours ago, he'd been filled with that silent fear that he'd have to risk going off-planet to find answers, even though he didn't know of any enemies outside humanity.

At least none willing to admit it.

Lots of humans who hated his guts. No shortage there.

Greyson circled back in his mind as he made his way on foot now, south and west for no better reason than he needed to move his legs and the weather was holding okay this afternoon. Gray and overcast, but not too windy. Not too cold.

Might even turn into a nice spring day when nobody was looking, although he wasn't holding his breath on that one. It was Boston, after all.

He checked his comm when his stomach rumbled. Early dinner worked, since he'd had a late breakfast and no lunch.

If a human chiptech like Laux really could make that chip, that eliminated a whole layer of misdirection from the case. Greyson wondered if whoever it was had built that logic into their plan, originally hoping that the shooter would have gotten lucky and killed Greyson, and that whatever detectives ended up investigating would fall for the obvious leads and head off-planet.

He smiled as his feet took him towards a little mom-and-pop joint specializing in Ghanaian food. He didn't come in here much because usually Rachel wanted Irish or Indian food when he asked.

But he was alone right now, and could do whatever he wanted.

It wasn't real Ghanaian food like you got in the old country. Nothing ever survived contact with American culture, even in this day and age. Folks came over for whatever reasons and wanted comfort food to keep them company. Eventually someone opened a restaurant, but had to buy things from American suppliers. Then locals discovered the joint, regardless of their own original ethnicity.

The American melting pot was the one everyone ate from.

But it was pretty good food and would hit the spot in his day.

The woman bustled out to his booth with a menu just as his comm beeped with a message.

Where are you? - Denise

Lovely. Greyson wondered if the Metropolitan had come up from DC this afternoon and been looking for him at the Bureau office. Denise Upkins tended to do things her way. That frequently involved sudden movements like that, just to keep people on their toes.

He thought about it and shrugged.

Just sat down for food.

He sent along the address, wondering if she'd demand he return to the office, or show up here. And if she'd have Edgar Redhawk, her personal assistant/political assassin, in tow. Probably drag Rachel along if she did.

ETA 5.

He nodded to himself, wondering what he'd done, or someone else, to light a fire under her ass.

Order me the Jollof rice with lamb.

Greyson chuckled. He'd wondered if she remembered this place, and a dinner date they'd had in the semi-mythical past.

Apparently so.

The waitress returned and Greyson explained that he had someone coming along in five to ten minutes. He ordered a sweet coffee for himself and dinner for the two of them.

Rachel or Edgar could sit at a different table and order their own damned food, but Greyson got the impression that they'd be outside in a stretch limo if they came at all, idling at the curb with those political plates that meant you couldn't issue them a parking ticket.

He passed the time by making a mental list of everyone who hated him enough to hire assassins. That was a long list, upon reflection, even eliminating dead people.

It was a much shorter list when he cross-indexed in all the names that could lay hands on his most recent ID photo from the Bureau files.

Dominguez was dead, killed originally by Ethen, even though Zaborra Strani, Ethen's bully of a partner, had gotten the official credit.

Now-former Boston Police Commissioner Buford Owens had managed to retire onto his pensions without prosecution, probably after doing a deal with Upkins to keep his mouth shut and maybe hand over whatever blackmail files he had accumulated.

Now-former Eastern North American Head Police Commissioner Yulia Kwan was another head that had rolled last fall when Denise had started paying attention to all those little, niggling rumors of corruption in the department. Kwan had been demoted and eventually took a transfer back to Vladivostok to live closer to her extended family. At least that was the public story. She also happened to be half a planet away if someone wanted to interview her about subordinates taking money under the table and maybe kicking things back to her along the way.

Greyson didn't think Kwan was as corrupt as Owens had been, but she didn't have white hands. None of them did.

Owens had just been promoted according to the *Peter Principle*, reaching his level of incompetence when he should have stayed a Police Commander. Still a political job, but a civil service one, where the union would hold its nose and protect you from hungry sharks like Metropolitan Denise Upkins on a bad day.

The only other name that stood out was the one he'd been circling for several days like bait hanging seductively off a hook.

Detective/Captain Olek Jan Zielinski, retired. Greyson's boss in the old days. A nasty little weasel of a man.

Zielinski was the kind of cop that forty-odd years later still referred to a President of the United States of America as "*that nigger*."

The man hated everyone that didn't look like him. Didn't talk like him. If you weren't Polack-American from Chicago, you were trash. Adding a bunch of alien species to the mix sixteen years ago had just meant that Zielinski had that many more kinds of people to insult and abuse. Colors and shapes beyond all the humans the man could oppress.

Zielinski hated them all. Still did, as far as Greyson knew.

It had probably been Zielinski's calling in life to join and help shape the Hunter Bureau when it got started. Greyson assumed that even a force with a reputation as bad as CPD had been happy to get rid of the man and all the problems an attitude like that probably brought to the concept of *community policing*. He was a rusty iron hammer when most of the time you needed a velvet glove.

The basic purpose of the Hunter Bureau was to make great hammers for any number of problems.

Greyson still liked to think of himself as a shiv. That was the army leftovers in his head. They'd trained him to handle those jobs because *they* could always call in airstrikes.

Sometimes politics necessitated that you use the edge of a razor, rather than the facing front of a claymore mine to solve your problems.

Zielinski might be worth solving with a claymore one of these days. Or a big sword.

Denise walked in before Greyson got too wound up on that thread of logic.

At fifty-four, she was still gorgeous. Tall black woman who dyed the grays away. Originally from Maryland. Widowed thirteen years ago. Two grown children and grandkids now.

She'd been a power figure in Boston and Northeast politics when he first encountered her as part of a case. Their political tumbles had turned into romantic ones a time or two and he still had good memories of the woman.

He wasn't sure it would have worked out, but things had been precluded before they got too engaged.

Greyson rose from his booth and went to kiss her on the cheek, but she turned into him as he did and it landed on her lips instead. And didn't settle for just being a peck.

In public, even.

Shit, what'd I do now?

But she was smiling. That evil grin that said she was up to no good and nobody was going to be able to stop her. Hopefully, she hadn't just given him the literal kiss of death.

This was Boston. Folks around here understood that concept.

Probably just as well he'd had to step out of her life seven years ago. She'd been poised to run for Metropolitan, the mayor/governor of the Eastern Metroplex of North America. Went on to win it and been reelected.

Greyson had too many secrets from his time in the Army to survive any sort of inquiries into his sordid past. Assassins didn't turn into public boyfriends of powerful politicians.

So they'd had a long, heartfelt conversation one night, over a bottle of good wine. Gone at it like bunnies until dawn. Then he'd walked away, turning into just another anonymous Hunter again as she got herself elected and occasionally dated actors and retired athletes. Famous people, like her.

But she was sitting across from him now in that same Ghanaian restaurant that had been one of their first dates. It was late afternoon and she was dressed like a lawyer, which she was.

Nothing about the woman right now suggested that she was the most powerful politician on this side of the Mississippi River or Atlantic Ocean.

Just a woman meeting her beau for an early dinner.

Anybody want to buy a bridge, while we're at it?

Greyson smiled neutrally as she ordered sweet tea and hit him in the face with the full force of her beauty and charisma.

Gods, this woman was amazing.

He made a note to never let her and Emmy meet, unsure how they'd kill him, just that he'd never survive both of them in the same room.

"Still keeping your usual schedule, I see," she offered as the waitress walked away to get drinks and probably deliver food.

"Until you can convince the bad guys to keep banker's hours, I'm kinda stuck with it," Greyson replied, unable to stop grinning at her.

"I talked to Rachel Asher briefly," Denise said in that off-hand manner that suggested it might have involved Chinese water torture or maybe a rack. "She mentioned that you had a few leads you were pursuing…?"

"Was just making a list of everyone who hated me enough to send an assassin in public," he replied with a little more lightness in his voice than the situation probably deserved.

"I could get you a copy of the phone book with a few pages torn out," she chuckled.

He shrugged. Not an entirely wrong assessment.

But most of those names just hated men and women with badges. Someone had given the perp his picture.

"So what brings you up, Denise?" he asked, as the waitress brought out two plates for them and then retreated.

"You had a conversation with Parsons that suggested that maybe you weren't the only target here," Denise said.

He hadn't spelled it out like that when talking to the Captain, but Metropolitan Upkins was a sharp woman. So was Rutherford Parsons. Both had to be in order to read the tidal currents after long enough in the trenches.

"Lot of change in the Bureau recently," Greyson said ambiguously as he started into his dinner, watching her do the same. "Plus, the perp had a picture in his pocket that nobody should have been able to get hold of. Someone's sending me a message, Denise, but I'm looking for all the misdirection they've added to the sauce."

"Like maybe they resent me promoting Rutherford Parsons?" she asked. "You didn't want the job. Actively threatened me with retirement if I offered it to you again, as I recall."

"Still don't want it," he reiterated. "Considered asking London if they have any openings when Rachel goes, just so she can be my boss for a while."

"Anything to get away from me?" she teased, but there was an edge under it that Greyson could hear.

He and Emmy didn't really have a thing. She had her life making money and changing the future. He was a Hunter who dealt with aliens doing bad things on Earth. They intersected frequently enough, for dinner, dates, or just wild sex, but that was an adult thing.

He'd already known that being a kept man wasn't for him. He'd eventually get restless and cause trouble. Emmy understood that and didn't press.

Greyson wasn't sure where Denise might fit into all that. But her tone suggested that she remembered that date, so many years ago. This place. Wistful, maybe?

He smiled at her.

"You let me know when we live in a world where your career would survive someone paying a journalist to dig into my distant past," he said honestly. "Hell, even you being here in public with me and none of your aides might make this look like enough of a date that someone asks."

"You're the lead detective on a specific portion of a political case," she said, face turning serious even as her eyes continued to twinkle. "Of course, I need to occasionally be briefed by you. Not a euphemism, mind you."

He smiled and shook his head. She had kissed him. In public. But Denise was in rare form tonight. Feisty and quick-witted. The best kind of woman.

"Well, if you're feeling adventurous..." He just left that dangling out there and took another bite.

Her eyes got big for a second, then turned shrewd. Like maybe she'd almost expected him to proposition her for old time's sake, and then they got political.

"What evil are you up to, Greyson?" she asked, much more subdued now.

"I'm pursuing the alien tech aspect of the case," he also dropped his voice. She nodded. "Had a meeting with a contact today who suggested that maybe it was bleeding edge chiptech, but something they might be able to replicate, just knowing that it had been done."

"Your contact human?" she pressed.

He nodded.

"You should probably keep your findings merely theoretical, then," she said after a moment. "I was able to pull strings to get you involved, in spite of the fact that you're a target here, *because* it might be an alien thing."

He nodded a second time. He had offered her a way to take him off the case. Or for him to get himself removed if he chose.

Denise wanted him in the thick of it.

"So who's a target besides you?" she asked.

"Captain Rutherford Parsons, for one," he answered. "You might up her bodyguard detail for a while, but only with folks you and Edgar trust."

It was her turn to nod.

"And two?" she asked, but the look in her eyes already had that answer.

"*The Honorable* Denise Upkins, Metropolitan or the Eastern Metroplex," he said quietly. "This keeps feeling to me like an inside job, and that means all sorts of payback is possible, maybe for things we don't even know about. Owens, Kwan, and Zielinski are all at the top of my list right now, but I don't have enough evidence to justify publicly rattling their cages right now."

"What would it take?" she asked, suddenly deadly serious where she'd been flirtatious a moment ago.

Greyson leaned back now, food almost forgotten, and *considered*.

Two years ago, he'd been slowly rolling up all sorts of scumballs with strange contacts inside the Bureau. At some point, someone had panicked, and he'd been set up as the fall guy, unceremoniously fired and ostracized.

They'd taken his badge away from him. He'd burned all his ties.

The Army pension and a partial Bureau-issued one had left him with enough money to survive on comfortably, once he'd downsized his life, getting Liz to sell off his nicer books and put him in contact with a few folks for the other bits.

Smaller flat. Fewer monthly expenses.

A man who has never really attached himself to life

doesn't need much in the way of stuff. Too many years living out of a duffle bag or foot locker, and then later a police locker.

Murphy bed with a fold-down table. Sofa and a pair of comfortable chairs. The only expensive thing he had kept was that coffee maker. A good coffee maker, capable of going all the way down to Turkish when you needed it, that was a prize worth keeping.

Greyson supposed that Emmy might have stepped in after another six months or year and ordered him to do something with the rest of his life, but at that point he'd still been coasting along on a form of PTSD.

And then Zielinski had walked out of that drizzle and offered him his old job back.

"We have a leak in the Bureau," he finally said, centering himself on her now. "Down in Records. Maybe nothing, maybe not. The picture that the perp had in his pocket was my new ID photo when I came back. Whoever accessed that file is part of a chain that leads to someone, however twisted and obscure it might get."

"Thin, Leigh," she countered. "Any number of reasons why someone might have pulled that out of the records."

"It gives me a name," he smiled a Hunter smile at her now, thin and cruel. "Maybe a victim to lean on. Happy to rattle little cages on the way to big ones. Especially now."

She recoiled a little from the sudden vehemence in his voice.

Hell, he wanted to recoil, but he couldn't. The job required that he go after someone like a terrier going into the woodpile after a rat.

Someone had tried to kill him.

Greyson Leigh felt that it was only polite to return the favor.

[10]

RECORDS

As the old saw went, Closed Circuit Television cameras did not prevent crime. They solved them afterwards.

The crime happened. But angry cops like Greyson Leigh could track you forward and backward from that moment. Like a terrier on a rat.

Greyson didn't have a camera down in the records room. Hell, it wasn't even a room anymore. At some point, enough money had come along to take all those personnel records and make them electronic. Store them in a massive server room somewhere. Probably Worcester or someplace where the real estate and power would be cheap.

All you needed was fast, secured access and you could read them from anywhere with a positive signal.

But that necessitated security around them. After all, these were the complete lives of Earth Police Special Missions. More importantly, the Hunter Bureau. The dangerous folks.

So there was this little web angel sitting there listening and watching.

Greyson didn't think the thing was fully sentient. Even

the aliens were a little twitchy about making an electronic life form advanced enough to eventually demand rights.

But it didn't miss by much. You walked electronically into the lobby where this thing sat, like the world's meanest librarian, and asked for her to retrieve a file for you.

In the old days of paper files stored down in the basement, the officer on duty might accompany you back to the cabinets, but more likely he'd just wave you through and go back to his book.

All manner of mischief might result.

The Librarian didn't mind the exercise.

Greyson finished reading the technical specs of the information retrieval system and felt pretty comfortable about pursuing his next set of requests. He didn't want to leave his fingerprints in there, nor Rachel's.

Too easy to spook his rabbit.

So last night Edgar Redhawk had instead requested a paper printout of all the times a half-dozen personnel files had been accessed in the last six months. Greyson didn't figure that he needed to go back that far, but again, he and Denise were playing their own games of misdirection with whoever down in Records was still a little too bent.

Doing odd little favors for folks that they shouldn't. Not necessarily enough to be prosecuted, but probably enough to get you fired.

And blackballed. Hunter Bureau would happily tell people that you were never allowed to be rehired into their Records Division for any reason. Most organizations and agencies would draw their own conclusions from that sort of language.

He put the book reader down, still pretty sure that web angel wasn't sentient, and looked across the shared desk at Rachel.

The Bureau had evolved from local, state, and federal

policing agencies originally, and that included the furniture. Two desks slid together. If you needed to interview someone, you got a conference room, or a holding pen, so there weren't chairs.

Computer monitors were back to back. Old keyboards. Old mice. Old everything.

Greyson preferred reading on an oversized tablet. His eyes were still good enough that he didn't need any treatment or glasses, but that was a matter of time.

Probably. He might still be able to retain perfect vision for a long time, if he wasn't actually human under it all.

Rachel was doing paperwork, mostly because he had pulled rank this morning and made her do it instead of him. He'd review it all before signing it, but he had no doubts that it would be perfect.

Everything was a pop quiz with her, and she was always aiming for a perfect score.

He hadn't told his partner everything today. Partly, to keep her in the dark as a stalking horse. Greyson wanted to see who tracked on her, when she didn't know to deflect them.

She still wasn't as automatically paranoid as he was.

Yet.

Her comm chirped with a message. Greyson checked the time.

At least Redhawk was precise and predictable.

"Messenger downstairs with a package for us?" she looked up and asked quietly.

Greyson shrugged innocently enough and reached for his travel mug of coffee, hoping that it still had a few inches of sludge in the bottom to chew on.

Rachel rose and slipped her homework reader automatically into a pocket as she headed for the door.

Greyson sipped his empty mug like it had fluid and

glanced around the room, noting who looked up at Rachel as she walked by and how many of them were just staring at her ass.

She was twenty-three and something of a fitness nut. Jogging, lifting, stairs, yoga. It was a fantastic bottom and probably would continue to be for as long as he knew her.

Greyson knew all the rumors about the two of them sleeping together and didn't give two shits. For one, she was way too young for him. Two, she was too cop.

Three, she knew the truth about him. At least he thought so.

How do you confirm that someone knows your deepest, darkest, deadliest secret without actually asking them?

Greyson found that he was still a coward on that front. He'd rather live with a hint of fear than come right out if she didn't know and convince the woman that she needed to kill him.

But not everyone was watching her ass as it wiggled out the door and into the corridor. He made a mental note of names and then cross-indexed them back to Zielinski and others.

The game he was playing right now wasn't black and white. Police work never was.

Hunters generally had it easy that way. Your alien target is too dangerous, too sly, too slippery for the average cop to handle, so you brought in a killer to deal with them. Not every case ended in a termination, but every single case started with that as a possible outcome.

Two years ago, he'd been slowly rolling up all those little fishies outside the Bureau that had seemed to be a little too in-the-know. Bribery. Kickbacks. Accidental data breaches that happened to warn a suspect with just enough time to disappear, or at least destroy all the records that a warrant might seize.

Most of the big players had managed to get beyond his immediate reach, but that still left the little folk. Support staff with maybe too rich a lifestyle for their salary. People with interesting cousins who might be doing time in a federal prison for general naughtiness.

All sorts of issues.

Parsons hadn't wanted to completely destroy the Boston office when she took over, but Greyson had gathered from hints Denise had dropped last night at dinner that it had been a close thing.

Had he fallen on his sword and taken the promotion to Detective/Captain, Upkins might have fired everyone around here except Rachel and then temporarily transferred in folks from places like Houston or Miami until Greyson Leigh could reconstitute the Boston branch.

As if he didn't have enough enemies now.

At least Dominguez was dead. He'd been the worst, after Owens and Zielinski. The rest tended to just be gray figures coming and going. Mostly, ex-special forces, so knuckleheads who liked to solve problems with extreme firepower.

The exact opposite of Greyson Leigh along just about any axis you wanted to measure.

So he made a list of names. Caught chagrined glances his way, getting caught staring at Rachel's ass. Or maybe caught at other things.

He rose and took his travel mug with him. The coffee robots in the break room were crap, but he wasn't in charge of the budget to buy better ones.

That was about the only thing that might convince him to accept a Captaincy around here.

He washed out his mug and stuck it into the robot's maw, pushing buttons until the beast began its esoteric incantations. Conjuring the coffee gods and offering them sacrifices for the magic bean.

Greyson smiled at the image of himself as an old, Siberian shaman, out there on the steppes hunting demons.

Not all that different from his current job.

He grabbed his mug when it was done and wandered back to his desk.

At least they were in the opposite corner from the main door. Everyone hated that corner because it tended to be too cold, but it got him away from casual traffic. There was nothing achieving a greater industrial *ennui* than having to keep track of which sports seasons was happening right now and what had happened in the most recent game.

Yawn.

Rachel appeared again a few minutes later with a bundle. Honest to goodness old fashioned manila envelope, stuffed about two centimeters thick and stamped with "Level Five Security Only" on the front and back.

Rude, but he liked it. Rachel was a Two. Greyson only rated a Three.

Hopefully it was just an old package, and he didn't have to worry about the harridans in Records pitching a fit over him being in possession of it.

Or maybe he should be a shit and have a judge swear out a warrant for the whole thing, so he could enter it into the case file under Seal?

That would truly frost a few people.

Rachel knew he was up to something. She had been left here with Redhawk when Denise came for him last night.

Greyson wondered if Redhawk had delivered it himself. The man could be like that.

Rachel dropped it on his desk with a perfectly arched eyebrow, darker black on rich brown skin. Puerto Rican extraction babe cop who was tougher than most of the men in here. Meaner, too, if you didn't include Greyson Leigh on your list.

He smiled silently and reached for the package, noting that someone had taken the time to seal it up, rather than just stuffing the paper in.

Greyson paused and thought evil thoughts.

"I need coffee," he said, rising with a steaming mug in one hand.

"You have coffee," Rachel noted archly.

"You need coffee," he replied.

"I need coffee," she agreed with only the slightest eyeroll.

At least she understood his game. Most of it.

Better than the fools around them, trying really hard not to be obvious in their sidelong looks at the two of them and *some new development* in this case.

Now things were going to start getting interesting.

[11]
ACCESS

RACHEL DIDN'T GET OFF ON THE MIND GAMES WITH people in the same way Greyson did.

Sure, she got it. Understood what he was doing, but she had also realized that she was still a little too linear in her thought processes. Which was why she needed someone like Greyson Leigh as a teacher.

As he'd said, there wasn't anybody better at this sort of thing. Sneakiest bastard she'd ever met, that was for certain.

But she was learning.

He already had coffee. She needed coffee. Maybe tea. Maybe something flouffy in pink. Keep them guessing.

Whoever *they* were. She got that part, too.

Because this was all just a performance for the witnesses. That was why they'd only walked as far out the front door as the corporate chain shop on the corner, instead of getting in a car and driving clear to the South End or North Shore and finding a dive where she'd feel safer with the palmstunner in her hand, maybe both tucked in a pocket.

Maybe not.

The sort of joint where they marked you as a cop when you were still parking the car out in back.

She knew a few of those. Greyson had introduced her to a few more.

Boston had only gentrified so far in the last seventy years.

She went ahead and got herself a *Bingo*, just to be a shit. Chain had five little boxes printed down the side of the cup, where the person taking the order could specify things. Extra hot. Two pumps. Decaf. Coconut milk. No foam.

Check all five and you had yourself a bingo. Why the hell not?

All right, maybe she had her own games she played with strangers in coffee shops.

Greyson hadn't asked, so she hadn't volunteered that Upkins's personal aide, Redhawk, had been the one to hand her the package this morning. She'd thought that those two were headed home last night after the Metropolitan came back for the man at the office, but apparently they had stayed in town.

Or he had.

Bullet could get you to DC in a couple of hours if you needed, and it wasn't like you would ever be out of touch with the world on that train.

What had dinner been like with Leigh and Upkins? Rachel had never pried beyond what the man would volunteer. She knew that Leigh and Upkins had met outside of a professional context. Dated a few times several years ago. Still had an obvious chemistry if you watched them interact.

Greyson was too much of a bad boy for a woman like her, though. At least until she retired from the spotlight.

What would Emmy do on that day? Or would they share him?

Flights to London were pretty cheap on a semi-ballistic, if you didn't mind the shot of high-g getting there. Rachel figured from the way he was talking that retiring from Boston and heading east wasn't just a joke.

Leigh might want out. New life. New world.

New Greyson Leigh, but she didn't even think that too loud around the man. He just might be able to read her mind.

She watched him peel the sealed edge of the envelope and pull out a stack of papers.

"Most of that's crap, isn't it?" she asked quietly as he randomly cut the document stack and then reassembled it.

She was back to their first case together, when he did something similar to an oversized stack, just for a pair of cops who'd been watching them a little too closely from across a different restaurant.

"Most," he agreed with a hint of a grin. His voice was quiet under the pop music blaring over the noise of soccer moms, but she was used to reading his lips anyway. "Personnel files of the six of us working some aspect of this case."

"You looking for a rogue?" she asked slowly and carefully. He was pretty much reading her lips, too.

"Yeah, but it won't be here," he grinned again. Just a flash and gone.

She watched him work upside down as he flipped through sections and pages until he found whatever it was he was looking for.

Leigh pulled a single page out eventually and studied it closely for a long moment. Probably photographing it into long-term memory, knowing the man.

"Huh," he said after a moment, handing it to her with a half spin.

Rachel took it from his hand and studied it. Last six months showing every instance where someone had accessed Leigh's file.

Lot of traffic at the beginning, when he'd decided to finally keep the badge instead of telling them all to go piss up a rope. It fell to nothing five months ago.

She looked at the bottom and noted the most recent request came from Edgar Redhawk, *Office of the Metropolitan of the Eastern Metroplex*. Before that, a week of activity as he got assigned to the case and things got updated routinely from the system.

Most of the rest of it were just his work check-ins, showing him coming on duty and going off.

Except for one entry in the middle that stuck out like a sore thumb.

Rachel didn't even mouth the word, aware that Greyson Leigh's instincts had been correct.

Again.

What must it be like to live inside that man's head? Was she going to turn into a female version of Greyson Leigh one of these days? Did she care?

The job had always been paramount. Getting close. Getting hired. Getting to be a Hunter. Turning into management eventually. Maybe another Rutherford Parsons, or whatever the English equivalent was.

Good thing she was already watching British television shows in her spare time to find the right model for herself.

Rachel studied the name again and wondered. Detective/Hunter Fred Jansen. She remembered Leigh's take on the guy, but she'd never worked with the man on a case. Just seen him in meetings and turned down the occasional proposition for a date that felt more automatic than interested.

Jansen's a better killer, but he's not all that good a cop, a little too lazy to do all the legwork and building networks of informants.

Leigh's words, back on that first case she'd shared with him.

Sharp with a nerve scrambler, but not a man given to chess or other games of skill over luck.

Why had he accessed Greyson Leigh's personnel file four weeks ago? Other than to maybe get a copy of a picture that ended up in the pocket of a killer, she could not think of one good reason to do something so obvious, except that the case was supposed to be leading people off-planet by now.

Nobody would look.

They'd be after some alien factory on some offworld colony, turning out illegal, custom Synth Chips designed to let a human participate in his homicidal fantasies, except that he was acting it out with a live firearm, instead of seated comfortably in his living room, mentally masturbating in privacy.

You can hide in plain sight if nobody is looking for you.

She felt a chill come over her as she realized that Greyson was supposed to have ended up dead from that first ambush. Maybe her, too, except that she wore body armor.

But not the kind that would stop a .44 round at close range. Nobody used those. Just beams of various kinds.

Had Jansen set her up to die as well?

Rachel handed it back to Leigh with a growl she didn't bother suppressing.

He nodded in understanding.

Criminals frequently made mistakes. That was how they got caught.

It felt like a tiny thing. Subtle. Blink and you miss it.

Whoever it was should have done better to make sure Leigh hadn't survived that first encounter.

Because now she was angry, too.

[12]
JANSEN

THE NIGHT WAS COOL AND DRIZZLY AS GREYSON PULLED to the curb and studied the building down a block and across. Older neighborhood. Somewhat poor in an era where everyone was still recovering from the dislocations of the aliens arriving. Lot of older cars on the street, some of them predating the arrival.

Greyson didn't figure all of them ran, but people would hold on to them as long as they could. Buildings were the same way. Old and a little shabby but the place they had always called home. Smells from dinners cooked with a lot of grease would stick to the walls, even though the night was chill and damp in places. They would be there if he rolled his window down to sniff. Some things probably would last until the buildings were torn down.

Greyson had considered all the different ways he might approach this situation. Fred Jansen had been just another Detective/Hunter in the Boston office. Not as flashy as Dominguez or some of the others. Not as quiet as Greyson was.

A man doing what he needed to get by, but not much

more. Greyson could sympathize, but he'd only started doing that after he'd gotten himself fired and had nothing to do with his days.

Jansen was still a Hunter. Training. Running the streets. Working with various departments around New England when they needed his expertise.

Not many people out there specifically trained to kill aliens, after all.

Greyson turned to Rachel, waiting patiently in the passenger seat.

"Straight up like a bull in a china shop?" she asked.

"People make mistakes when they panic," he replied. "Don't even really want him as prey, so much as watching which way a man like Fred Jansen runs when he feels the walls suddenly start closing in."

"Who do you think he'll lead you to?" she asked, growing more interested now.

More focused.

Anybody but Rachel, he might have said aroused, but he didn't think *The Kill* was the sort of thing that turned her on.

Not that he'd ever asked.

More lethal instead, maybe.

"I have a list," Greyson said. "Half the names are just John and Jane Doe, one through whatever."

"And the other half?"

"People you might remember," Greyson admitted grudgingly.

"How many of them used to have badges like ours?" Rachel pressed.

"Most," Greyson said simply. "Just don't know which one might be our mastermind."

"You think there'll be fingerprints to trace?" she asked, unbuckling her harness now in prep for the stalk itself.

"We're supposed to be dead right now," Greyson

reminded her. "And other detectives are probably already on a starship to someplace where they can trace dead ends to a factory that never made these chips in the first place."

"Unless one of them is being set up as part of a side gig," Rachel smiled.

"Maybe," Greyson granted. "Maybe they're subtle enough to insert that, but I'm willing to bet you a toonie that anything you find is a red herring at this point."

"Then why bother?" Rachel asked.

Greyson unbuckled as a way to gain a few moments to think.

"Misdirection at the top level," he said. "Remember, that they had my picture says there are inside connections. That's the only thing here that feels real. The rest is all just bullshit designed to send people off after crap leads until the case grinds down to dead ends, because you missed the important elements at the beginning."

She started to open the door and paused, turning back to him with a fierce look.

"Does Jansen know he's been set up?" she asked. "Or is he another red herring? Maybe a fall guy for someone? Does he start shooting immediately or run?"

"That's why we're here," Greyson said, opening the door. "That's his favorite bar down the block. Fred never had much of a social life, as I recall. Sits and watches the game, whatever game it is, and drinks cheap beer. If we knock on his door at home, it's automatically a hostile situation. Fred's a killer, when he needs to be. He's just not a particularly deep thinker."

"So we just walk in like neighbors and say hi?" Rachel opened her door and looked around as she stood up. "What's he likely to do?"

"Panic," Greyson smiled as he joined her on the sidewalk and started walking. "Run, if we're lucky."

"Lucky?" Rachel asked.

"Honest men got no reason to bolt, Rachel," Greyson reminded her. "That's almost as good as a verbal admission of guilt, if that's what you're looking for."

He watched the impact of those words on her face. Just like her backing him accidentally into a corner and getting Greyson to admit that getting on a starship might be a bad idea.

Rachel flinched pretty hard and looked up at him with a glimmer of awe that she quickly suppressed. Greyson wondered how long they would dance around the topic of his humanity before she finally confronted him.

To outsiders, it would probably have the look and feel of an unspoken seduction and romance, like out of one of those romance books she was reading. The ones with a cop and an alien.

He suppressed his own shudder. Rachel didn't need the weirdness of a real cop/alien relationship on top of everything else.

She turned a stone face forward and walked. Greyson did the same, wondering how it might look to a random stranger. If the sexual tension appeared thick enough to stop a nerve scrambler beam to anyone else.

They continued in silence.

The front door of the neighborhood bar was glass, covered over with stickers and ads for beers and things that someone had stuck on both the inside and outside over the years.

Decades?

He pulled the heavy door open and felt the dull roar of conversation spill out over him, along with the smell of tobacco and other things you smoked. Bodies that hadn't had a shower today. Clothes maybe on their second day as well.

Grime, in all its flavors, wafted out on the warm air from inside as it blew in his face.

At one time, smoking had been everywhere. Then they tried to eliminate it indoors, driving the smokers out into the snow or rain for their fix.

Eventually, the forces of abstention lost all their momentum and enforcement of the prohibition of tobacco or marijuana today was mostly honored in the breach. A secondary charge that a cop might add on if you were being a pain in her ass for something else.

The killing blow had been vaping, about the time he was a teenager experimenting with youthful rebellion. Fluid in a charged chamber that you sucked down into your lungs and absorbed.

Almost as bad as tobacco, at the end of the day, but harder to detect unless you went all strident on people.

Not worth the effort.

The inside of the bar had some pretty hardcore fans sucking at the smoke and vape fumes. It hit Greyson like a blanket of wet dog fur when he stepped in.

The noise of the fans wasn't all that rude, but it would cover a lot of conversation, especially with the basketball game blaring from every corner of the place.

He stepped in and looked around. Bar on his left behind the basic rope separator to keep juveniles at bay. Kitchen beyond the end of the bar. Tall and short tables down his right. Longer tables tall enough for bar stools or standing, back on the right. Hallway beyond everything, leading to the bathrooms, if Greyson had to guess.

Only so many ways to arrange a space like this, and bars tended to run cheap on interior decorating. Except for all the electric light beer logos, what people who had no chemistry background called neon.

Rachel was right behind him as he started forward,

counting noses down the bar, since most of the stools were full.

He was just about to the bar itself, and the tall woman tending, when movement on his right caught his eye.

Greyson turned to see Fred Jansen standing in that back hallway, like he'd just come out of the bathroom and frozen.

They made eye contact and Greyson watched the man's face turn white. Fred's eyes got huge.

He turned and bolted for the back door without a word.

"Fuck!" Greyson barked under his breath.

Just about as good as a verbal admission of guilt.

He'd really hoped that Fred was only tangentially guilty. Maybe done a favor for someone without any understanding of what the long-range implications might be.

But Fred seemed to be in it up to his neck.

Greyson turned and started running, bouncing off a stranger who had just stepped the wrong way. The man turned with a curse and growled at Greyson.

A fist started back, when Rachel stuck a gun in the man's face.

"Hunter Bureau business," she snarled up at him, like a Chihuahua threatening a grizzly bear, flashing her badge at him. "Move or bleed."

Not exactly the most subtle way to do it, but the stranger flinched under the tone. Or the palmstunner she held in her hand with the calm certainty that he was only worth shooting because he was in her way.

Her look promised that he'd be like shit she needed to wipe off her boots afterwards.

She might have been spending too much time around ex-Army assassins.

Or something.

Greyson nodded a polite understanding to the grizzly bear and slid past him, only accelerating when he was clear.

Other heads had turned this way, but nobody rose from their stool. No hands vanished into pockets for a weapon.

Greyson drew his own palmstunner now and pursued.

He would be fine shooting anything right now.

He could always apologize later, if he had to.

From the way Fred Jansen had bolted, Greyson didn't figure that would be necessary.

[13]
RUNNER

Rachel was off in Greyson's wake, pausing only enough to put her badge away because the tables were too close together for her to keep up.

Nobody in the place wanted to be shot tonight, which was good. She wasn't feeling charitable. Especially not that big punk.

Jansen hadn't even asked what they were up to. Just run at first sight. She hadn't spotted the man until he turned and went for the back door.

They were out that door now.

Dark alley with a few pools of light where she figured she'd find cooks having a smoke during a quiet stretch of the evening. Maybe just bums tonight.

Other bums. The kind that didn't even have enough sense to live in one of those cribs the government would make available for you.

Some people simply refused to be helped.

Not that Rachel Asher had any idea what that might be like.

Movement in this alley was going to draw fire. That was the joy of a palmstunner.

Up ahead, Greyson was moving faster than a fifty-year-old should be able to, but he had been in good shape when she first met him, running up and down stairs instead of taking elevators, just for the work out.

Now, nobody knew what good shape would mean.

She had youth and rage on her side, and could keep up. Jansen was the one she'd be expecting to run out of gas first.

In that fool's mind, he probably figured he only had to run faster scared than Greyson Leigh could chase him angry, not understanding just how fast angry might be tonight. And Rachel didn't figure she had the will that Leigh did.

A shadow exited the alley on the left onto a street.

Leigh was already after him. Rachel followed, drifting a little to her left as she did.

Palmstunner had a greater range than a nerve scrambler did, and she didn't want Jansen to be hiding in a dark spot just around a corner on them, where they might get close enough that he could shoot them both before they could react.

Rachel considered running with the nerve scrambler in her off hand, but that would suggest malice aforethought later, rather than the heat of the moment. Plus, she needed her right hand free for doors or whatever else.

Like punching people.

For an old guy running, Greyson moved on silent feet, but she'd heard enough about his youth to understand just how lethal the man had been at her age. She was happy just keeping up.

Jansen was the one losing ground.

They got to the corner and Greyson slowed abruptly. She was feeling rambunctious, so she went wide around the corner, wondering if she was drawing fire for her partner. And if it would hurt.

Dark street. Side street kind of place, where light industry closed up chain link fences at night. The kind of barriers topped with loops of razor wire to keep the tweakers from climbing over and causing property damage.

No beams in her direction.

Whew.

Jansen hadn't decided to make a last stand.

Not yet anyway, she amended the thought.

Man still seemed of the opinion that he could get away from them.

From her.

From an angry Greyson Leigh.

Yeah, good luck with that, princess.

Rather than bunch up, Rachel went ahead and looped wide as she gave chase, crossing the street between a pair of parked cars to the far side of the road.

What did Fred drive?

They hadn't stopped to run that information, afraid that it might tip off whoever else back in the office might be on Fred's side.

At least enough to warn him that Greyson Leigh was coming.

Rachel had never really felt like a lethal gun moll, at least until she saw the anger in Greyson's face when he'd figured out who might have set him up.

Deadly as she was, that man pretty much made her look like a bantam facing a heavyweight in an open card bout.

Ugly, messy, and about to be painful.

She glanced back and caught movement as Greyson pursued on his side of the street. Jansen had his head down and was running like Hell itself was on his heels.

Not the most inapt metaphor, all things considered.

Fred was running loudly, too, shoes slapping leather on the drizzle-wet pavement. In fact, the drizzle was getting heavier as she watched.

Rachel wondered what a full-out rain might do to the range of a palmstunner.

There were weapons you could requisition when you were expecting weird weather. Beams designed to keep a tighter focus in rain and snow, range at a cost of accuracy. She hadn't thought about it until now because they were only here to question Fred about some things that had looked awkward in the light of day.

Right?

Except that he'd run as soon as he'd seen them.

Bullets didn't really give much of a shit about weather. Maybe she should qualify on a slug-thrower sometime? Except that nobody would certify her to carry one in the field. Too much risk of innocent bystanders getting hurt.

That was what the palmstunner was for.

Maybe she needed to see if there was something for Boston winters, and start carrying that? Heavy stunner with the nerve scrambler's battery pack?

Fred ducked around a corner up there by more or less doing a parkour thing to run partly up the far wall and use that as a pivot. Pretty impressive.

He wasn't as old as Leigh. Older than her. Still in good shape and it took a lot of training to pull that, unless blind terror was lending him reflexes.

Fred had about a block head start on them, so Rachel put her head down and tried to close the gap.

She looked over and Greyson was gone.

Rachel didn't think he'd turned invisible. At least she really *really* **really** hoped that whatever he was these days couldn't do that.

Probably ducked down the block back at the same time Fred had turned left up here.

Good. Catch him in a crossfire. Or something.

Rachel had no backup right now as she was running down her perp, but that was nothing new. Dominguez had always been a lover, not a fighter. He'd have probably lost the race by the end of that first alley, except that Carlos wouldn't have tried to ambush Fred like this in the first place.

Would have shown up at his door and knocked. Or maybe walked up in the office, or at the coffee machine.

What sort of explosive confrontation would have resulted? Certainly not this sort of admission of guilt, if that was what this was. Box him maybe, where he could just brush everything off and they'd be no closer to an answer?

Greyson Leigh didn't play nice.

Rachel was a good student.

Because she had a kitty-corner intersection to work with, she went right out diagonal, weaving a little until she could see. All these streets were narrow and a little twisty, going back to the cattle and sheep trail days when Boston was a tiny place.

And they changed names every three blocks for fifty kilometers, but she figured they did that just to mess with anyone not born here. Bostonians could be like that. They all still called themselves Massholes on any given day.

Some instinct warned her.

Rachel threw herself down and to one side as the beam flashed out of the night.

Cops were trained to shoot center body mass. With a beam, you had more flexibility than a bullet, because of how it attenuated at range. A bullet cut a path no bigger than her finger.

And the rain was doing weird things to the beam. Diffracting it almost, so it was twice as wide. Probably still hit like a bitch if it touched her, but she could see a million tiny rainbows as it crossed the drizzle.

At least that stupid son of a bitch hadn't gone for his own nerve scrambler. She'd give him the benefit of the doubt on that, since that was a guaranteed lethal shot unless she got absolutely dead lucky at every step after that.

Rachel had trained how to fall. Part of staying in shape.

It was awkward and messy, the way she did. Jacket was probably ruined, if that was cloth tearing. Bruises galore tomorrow from the hard way she landed.

But he missed.

Stupid son of a bitch was dead meat now.

Rachel still had her pistol. She fired randomly on Jansen's rough direction now, not quite sure where he was, but not trying to do anything but force the man's head down.

Greyson was out there somewhere.

Hunting.

She popped off a second shot and kind of continued her tumble across the wet roadway, hoping like hell that there weren't any half-blind drunks out tonight rumbling these back streets to stay away from the cops.

She'd get her stupid ass run over before she knew what happened.

Parked car. Illegal, since it was too close to the intersection, but she wasn't about to complain as it gave her cover from the night.

Unless Jansen was coming at her now and circling, she had a second to catch her breath.

And Greyson had that much longer to get beyond the man.

It was uncharitable to think about the things Leigh might do to a bent cop, but she wasn't feeling all that much love for her fellow man right now.

She got her feet under her and looked through the windshield, but couldn't see Jansen or anybody else.

At least she wasn't trying to do this at rush hour. He'd have already gotten away from them at that point.

Except where was Fred Jansen going to run to? She hadn't thought that far ahead, any more than he probably had.

Guilty conscience and boom, out the back door.

Dumb-ass.

She popped to her feet, sniffing downrange with the palmstunner.

Empty streets.

He hadn't gone past her, and she had this intersection covered, so he must be going deeper into whatever industrial complex this all represented.

She was up and giving chase again.

Maybe a little more careful.

Maybe not.

They both had nerve scramblers tucked away. Rachel hadn't drawn hers because the range on them sucked. Probably the same for Fred.

She thought about it as she moved.

There was nobody about.

Not Jansen. Not Leigh.

Not even winos meandering around at nine at night in the rain.

Just a wet, sore, angry Rachel Asher and her gun.

Hopefully, she wouldn't shoot a cat. They might not be strong enough to handle a palmstunner, and then they'd be down to eight.

Or whatever.

There. Movement.

Rachel took off again, hoping that it was Jansen she was after and not some punk panicked at beamfire.

He turned a corner and Rachel saw enough of his face in the distance to confirm that it was Jansen.

She had him now.

There is a particular sound rubber tires make, skidding loosely across wet pavement. Kind of a squeal with percussion because the tires bounce loose a little and then grab again.

She heard that.

A moment later, someone threw an orchestra down a flight of stairs, bass drum first, followed by trumpets.

It took her a moment to organize the sounds into coherence. Maybe she'd rung her own bell on the ground and not realized she had a mild concussion or something?

Rachel ran to the corner, chasing Jansen and confirmed what had happened.

There was a big-ass truck stopped in the middle of one of those narrow streets. The grill was dented inward pretty hard, from where the driver hadn't been able to stop in time.

And had slammed into Fred Jansen at speed.

Greyson appeared on her left now as she got to the body lying in the street. She got a hand on his neck and confirmed a pulse, even as she holstered her pistol and grabbed her comm.

Two clicks and she had the emergency channel. The encrypted one that let the Bureau teams talk without civilians listening in.

"I have emergency traffic," she said as the operator came on line.

"Go ahead," the man said.

Rachel fed him the intersection, looking up at the sign.

"Officer down," she continued. "He stepped off a curb and was blindsided by a truck. Unconscious and I have a pulse. Need medical teams here immediately."

"Rolling now," the man said. "ETA four minutes."

Fred Jansen was a mess. Blood everywhere.

Thank God he'd been high enough that the bumper and grill had gotten him, instead of managing to fall under tires and get utterly squished.

Greyson leaned close as he walked by.

"I have his pistol," the man muttered. "Good call on EMS."

Rachel didn't know what to do at this point, so she rolled him enough onto his side so that he wouldn't accidentally drown in his own blood or the rain.

He was moaning, but she figured that was a good sign, all things considered.

Greyson was talking to the driver, who looked to be in almost as bad a shape as Jansen, but who goes to work and expects to run over someone who comes off a curb at full speed?

But maybe she could get some answers this way.

[14]

HOSPITAL

Greyson was seated in the waiting room, meditating on his many sins. Rachel was the only other person here, sitting next to him and reading her homework, as usual, still a little damp and more than a little pissed at the world.

They were in an isolated wing, off from the main part of the hospital and quiet, but it still had that old industrial feel. Every hospital waiting room seemed cut from the same mold. Tile floors in a black and white checkerboard. Paint white above his waist and sand below. Hanging ceiling. Smell of over-roasted coffee stuck to the chairs and sofas around here.

Rutherford Parsons came through the outside door like a tornado. She was dressed for an evening out, in a slinky, emerald evening gown with a wrap, and not in her pretty, blue uniform that they all wore for dress occasions, so he figured he'd ruined her evening on top of everything else, but Greyson wasn't sure if he should put that in the win column or not.

Edgar Redhawk was on her heels, but he didn't see Denise.

Probably for the best.

The Captain took the whole scene in with those hard, glacial-blue eyes and Greyson felt the weight of them descend on him.

The room was currently empty as far as Greyson's eyes or ears had been able to track anyone. It was the hospital, sure, but in a wing dedicated to special circumstances. Like wounded cops or high-value prisoners.

Nobody around, and even the nurses and doctors didn't stay around any longer than they needed to. All anybody had to know was that Fred Jansen was a Hunter, and had been hit by a truck.

The staff here could handle the rest. At least the medical bits.

Greyson was handling the other problems.

Redhawk closed the door while Parsons watched, then checked the inner door back to the operating theater.

Greyson measured the woman.

Tough. That was the word he'd use for Parsons, if he only had one. Political would be the second.

Not an assassin like Redhawk, but not a bureaucrat like Owens had been.

Possibly the second most honest cop Greyson knew after Rachel.

"My briefing was probably inadequate," she said abruptly, nodding to Redhawk as he came to rest.

Where she was big in personality and physicality, Redhawk was—not small, but Greyson didn't have a good word to describe the man.

Forty-something, and that was as much detail as he ever let on to, and only then because he understood some of the old jokes kids like Rachel didn't get. Black hair, representing his Sioux heritage. Skin a little darker than Rachel's. Five eleven, maybe. Forgettable face, but on purpose.

Deadly in an emotionally-compact way. He'd been Owens's right-hand hatchet man before the Commissioner overstepped his bounds and got thrown to the wolves. Redhawk had worked for Denise since.

As capable an operator as they came, and that was saying something.

"He didn't have all the details, because I don't even trust the encryption around here to hold," Greyson replied.

Rachel slipped her reader into her pocket. She looked like a drowned raccoon that had just climbed out of a trash can, but hadn't had any interest in running home to get clean or a change of clothes.

At least not until after this confrontation was over.

"Tell me," Parsons ordered in that quiet voice she had.

One of the other things Greyson liked about the woman.

No bullshit. She wasn't any tougher than her Hunters, but also wasn't trying to constantly convince you she was.

Zielinski had been an asshole that way.

Greyson also nodded to Redhawk.

"I asked him to get me some files last night," Greyson began as Parsons grabbed a nearby chair and sat, rather than towering over him in a Statue of Liberty kind of way.

"Was it in there?" Redhawk suddenly asked.

Greyson tended to forget what a nice voice the man had —soothing, fit for radio—because Redhawk spoke so little, and when he did they tended to be threatening words, at least for other people.

"It was," Greyson replied, turning his attention back to Parsons, and wondered again if she'd been called out of the opera or some other fancy event to come to the hospital for one of her men.

She just studied him.

"The files on the six of us working prime on this case," Greyson continued. "As a cover. I wanted to see who might have accessed my personnel file to get that picture that the shooter had."

Parsons nodded now.

On top of everything else, Rutherford Parsons was a damned good cop. And a former street-level Hunter in her own right.

Another role model for Rachel to watch. To learn from.

"Jansen," she stated, rather than asking the obvious question.

"The only name that didn't have a perfect alibi," Greyson agreed.

"Tell me what happened tonight," she ordered.

Greyson began, getting her up to the moment he'd turned left and started circling the block. Rachel had to take up the thread now, filling in details he didn't even know.

She also got to explain how she came by the drowned rat look and the bruises.

The right side of her face was starting to look like a night of really rough sex from the way it was red and starting to turn purple where she'd hit the ground hard.

Greyson had taken the report from the guy driving the truck, but that man hadn't been able to say much. Just driving down the road to make his next delivery when somebody darted out from between two parked cars and right into the hood ornament of his Peterbilt beast before he could shut it down.

Bounced at least far enough not to be squished, which really was what mattered right now. Greyson could only imagine the shitshow that would have resulted from an accidental death.

And it would have been accidental. He was at pains to make sure that he hadn't fired at all, and that Rachel had only returned fire to scare Jansen off, after he had started it.

"Why?" Parsons finally demanded after he sat for several lonely minutes and digested the whole.

"Somebody hates me enough to go through all that effort," Greyson replied, starting his explanation at the top level. "But they had contacts in the Bureau, which suggested to me that it was more than just that. Maybe there is someone out there who hates you almost as much. Or maybe Denise. Maybe all of us."

"All that from a name on a file access?" She almost sneered the words.

"I was there to talk to Fred off-property," Greyson said. "Get him on neutral ground that would favor him, maybe to get the man a little more relaxed than doing it at the office or just showing up at his front door. He bolted the moment he saw me. No words. No questions. Boom, out the back door. Didn't slow down. Fired on Rachel when he realized that we were in better shape than he was and that we'd eventually run him down."

"What game are you playing, Leigh?" Parsons pressed.

"Something Rachel pointed out to me early on in this case," Greyson smiled grimly at the three of them. "Getting a suspect to admit to a crime without saying anything. Just by putting them into the right situation and watching their body language before they can control a flinch."

"And Jansen flinched," Parsons completed the thought.

Greyson nodded.

More words were interrupted by the inner doors bursting open suddenly and a woman in off-green scrubs entering the room. She was the surgeon, Greyson was guessing, based on the blood splatters on her arms and chest.

Greyson stood and she locked hard on him, quick-scanning the other three and ignoring them.

"Leigh?" the doc asked.

"That's right," he nodded to her.

Short and a little heavyset. Looked Japanese by way of five or so generations in Hawaii of California, but he was just going on the bones in her face.

"Your boy will survive," the doctor said. "Miracles of modern medicine notwithstanding, he got lucky ten ways from Sunday. Broken arm. Broken leg. Several cracked ribs. Fractured skull. Concussions, contusions, and just about everything else, but we got to him in time. I've put him into a medical coma for a few days, just because we had to open him up in so many places to fix things, and there are limits to what even the best of the alien medicine can do for the man. But he should make a full recovery and be ready to briefly take visitors by Monday if everything works out right between now and then."

"Thank you," Greyson said simply.

Working with pros was lovely. Come in, deliver all the information he needed in a single breath.

"He's also in a secured part of the hospital, so I'll need your people to send over a list of all the visitors he's allowed, as well as provide a contact for any unexpected relatives that come out of the woodwork."

"Understood," Greyson nodded. "There's nothing we can or need to do tonight?"

"Not the first time we've had one of your people, Detective/Hunter," she flashed him the first smile he'd seen from the woman. "The protocols are all written down."

"In that case, we'll get out of your hair," Greyson said.

He started to reach for one of his business cards and thought better of it. Parsons didn't have anywhere to hide a business card carrier. At least, not that didn't require showing off more of her flesh than Greyson wanted to see right now in order to pull it out.

"Rachel, can I get one of your cards?" he said to his

bedraggled partner. "You'll be the point of contact until the Captain sorts it all out."

He nodded to the tall woman, and included Redhawk in that. There would be conversations outside this room, and they might get a little loud. Greyson didn't figure he would be involved in many of them, because he was already so deep into the mess that nobody would expect that he could be objective.

Outsiders, that is. Hunters would know, but Parsons would be playing a political role, as much as she might want to do otherwise.

Rachel rose and gave him a dirty look as she handed the doc a card.

Greyson had enough interesting women in his life already. Denise had held onto his card and called him after that investigation was over. So had Emmy.

This was not a scavenger hunt, regardless of the appraising look the doc gave him. The secret smile that said she had been thinking exactly of calling him up in a month or two and inviting him out for drinks or something.

Or something.

The doctor vanished back into the innards of the hospital and Greyson found himself at the center of the other three.

"Now what?" Parsons asked, studying him with hard eyes. "Or am I better off pretending I don't know anything so I have plausible deniability later, Leigh?"

"Jansen is a thread connecting the folks in Records to whoever hired an assassin," Greyson replied. "I doubt he's the one who had it in for me. He's too lazy to build a conspiracy. And too dumb to look around when someone else is building one and using him, if I had to be an asshole on the topic."

"Who are you going after next?" Redhawk spoke up now, nodding to Parsons as she stepped slightly back.

Physically isolating herself, as it were.

"Considering the four of us and what we represent, I have three candidates in mind," Greyson said. "But I don't have enough information in hand to ask for warrants yet."

Parsons nodded at that and immediately turned for the outside door, stiletto heels clacking as she walked.

"Edgar, keep me posted," she called over her shoulder, and then was gone.

Greyson grinned. One down. The hard one, too. The honest cop, because Rachel was almost as angry as he was now.

"Short trip, long trip, or local?" Redhawk asked now.

Florida, Vladivostok, or the North Shore?

Zielinski, Kwan, or Owens?

"We have a few days before Jansen is awake and able to contact whoever it is to give them warning that I'm coming." Greyson felt his smile turn shark-like. "Given leaks, I'd rather not ask for a judge to sign off on a warrant right now, even under seal, so I'm just going over to Fred's place to pick up some clothing and things for him. You know, friendly face around the office, since he doesn't have a wife or girlfriend that we're aware of."

"Beware of admissibility," Redhawk warned him.

"If this goes down the way I think it will, it probably won't end in a criminal prosecution, Redhawk," Greyson warned the man back. "Jansen was truly an unforeseen accident. A fool who should have known better, but got in over his head doing a favor for a friend. Probably only guilty of things that leave a letter of reprimand in his file and nothing more."

"And his friends?" Redhawk asked.

"They're going down hard," Greyson promised. "The kid gloves are off. If I end up protecting Rutherford and Denise in this, that's accidental, because somebody wanted me dead and I see no reason not to return the favor."

Redhawk studied him for a long moment and then nodded to some inner conversation.

"Don't brief me," he said abruptly. "Just file your regular reports and I'll pull out the pieces I need for Denise from that. I'd appreciate if your first call was my way, before you called for EMS or backup, just so we can set the right firewalls at our end. Nothing personal."

"No offense taken," Greyson said. "We're all adults here."

Redhawk nodded, smiled to Rachel, and left.

Greyson turned to Rachel. Noted the anger coming off the woman like steam.

"Let's get you cleaned up," he said. "We need to move quickly."

[15]

BREAKING AND ENTERING

GREYSON KNOCKED QUIETLY ON THE DOOR, JUST IN case someone really was there and would answer. Or to scare off whoever was already breaking into Jansen's flat before he got there to do the same thing.

After a moment, he pushed the key he had taken from Fred's personal items into the first lock and started undoing them. He'd get the ring back to the hospital long before Fred needed them.

Like many people Greyson knew, Jansen had three locks set in the door. The knob one that came with the place, plus a deadbolt that might and might not have a decent strikeplate. Then the other one, set at eyeball level later by the tenant with a solid plate. The kind that would hold against anything but a team of cops with a ram and a running start.

Rachel watched the hallway, but managed to look casual about it. That was pretty good acting on her part, considering how angry the woman still was every time he caught her reflection in something.

Nobody on this floor stuck their heads out to see, but

this was the kind of neighborhood that might not call the cops if they heard screaming in the back alley. Rough place.

Why Jansen chose to live here wasn't clear, but Greyson remembered from somewhere that Fred had been at this address for more than a decade. Like so many other things about the man, maybe he was just too lazy to change until it was forced upon him.

This place made more sense if you were on a rookie cop's salary, before making it to Detective in the Hunter Bureau.

The final lock surrendered and Greyson automatically reached back for his palmstunner. Behind him, he caught a quickly-suppressed snort from Rachel as he slipped the key ring into his pocket.

"Really?" she whispered.

Greyson went ahead and did it anyway, opening the door and entering behind the barrel.

He already knew he was dealing with trouble, just not the shape it would take. And he didn't know anybody he could ask about Fred's personal life without tipping somebody off that the game was moving forward.

So palmstunner instead of nerve scrambler. At least he could apologize later if he had to.

Or wanted to.

Greyson reached in and flicked on the hall lights as Rachel turned to follow him.

Entryway. Same linoleum floor as the hall outside. Lasted forever and could be cleaned with a mop or a robot. Ugly, faux-wood paneling on the walls that had been briefly in style in the late Thirties. About the time a young cop named Jansen might have first moved in.

Living room on the left of the door. Dining room on the right with the kitchen behind it going back. All the furniture looked old and worn. Mismatched in that way that it did when something broke and you bought a replacement second hand from whatever they had in stock. Mostly wood, but stained in colors everywhere from honey down to walnut. Rugged looking, at least.

Greyson sighed quietly to himself as he moved out of the way for Rachel to enter. He closed the door and set the locks again.

Looking around, he mentally down-rated Fred Jansen another notch. Greyson had been hoping that the man was just a slob at work, and secretly had something more exciting going on at home. A hobby that he might obsess about. An interest beyond the latest sportsball season.

Something.

Anything.

Greyson had his synth whiskey and his classical music to keep him focused whenever he managed to be off duty. Books had once been a thing. There would be something new whenever he finally got settled into being a Hunter again.

Anything but ties.

Rachel was forever doing homework, so reading and writing papers. Occasional classes, but the program she was in was built around a working cop's hours, which meant she was mostly studying at home until she was ready and then scheduling a test, rather than being on some professor's clock.

Fred Jansen's flat felt more like a hotel room. Generic prints on the walls that looked like something he'd picked up at a pawn shop. Mismatched. Couch worn from one butt but not two, lined up to face a screen on the wall separating the living room from the kitchen.

Nothing at all that gave the room flavor or even personality.

Greyson stepped past Rachel to glance into the kitchen before heading back into the living room. There was a hallway with a door on the right and the left facing each other, plus another one on the end he figured went to the one bedroom.

Both were open as he got closer, with the bathroom on the right, running across the back of the small kitchen. There was a linen closet on the left with a washer/dryer unit stacked in back, going to the outer wall of the flat.

The bedroom door was partly opened, so Greyson peaked in.

Studio style, stretching all the way across the width. Greyson could see a simple bed, double wide with a headboard and nightstand on this side. Clock. Lamp. Knick-knacks. Bad art.

Light from the hallway spilled in, so he pushed the door the rest of the way. Dresser lined up with the door, between a pair of windows that were covered.

The only interesting thing was the built-in vanity mirror and counter on the left wall, opposite the bed. Space for a woman to sit and do her morning rituals, if she wore war paint. Rutherford did. Rachel didn't.

Jansen had configured it as an office, with a large, laptop computer resting awkwardly on the space. Like you had to look yourself in the face while surfing on the computer.

Awkward, depending on your kinks.

Sliding door closet was in the back corner. Greyson started there.

Unlike Dominguez, Jansen lived a pretty mundane life outside the office as well as inside. Off-the-rack suits in muted colors ranging from boring green to boring black. White dress shirts. Footwear appropriate to all of Boston's seasons, but not nearly as combat-oriented as his or Rachel's.

She had followed him into the bedroom.

"Man lives like a monk," she said simply. "Worse than you."

"How so?" he asked her, turning to see what she had.

"I looked in the bathroom," Rachel grinned. "Bachelor stuff and way dirtier than yours. Nothing left behind by a woman, so she didn't probably come back more than once, if she ever existed. Plus, that bed's not wide enough for two to sleep comfortably. Even you have a queen-sized Murphy. Bachelor who's never lived with a woman and doesn't try to keep it clean enough for one to want to spend the night."

"Huh," he replied.

Made sense. He'd been under military jurisdiction, so everything was sharp at all times. Tucked, cleaned, and bounce a loonie off it at random inspections.

Jansen had stuff. Things on random shelves that he'd picked up somewhere, like Mardi Gras beads hanging from the post at the foot of the bed. Bobblehead dolls from local sports teams.

But he just slept here. Jansen didn't inhabit this space like Greyson did with his flat, or Rachel with her apartment.

Greyson wondered if the woman who had been tending bar was as close as Fred Jansen was ever getting to having a wife. He'd have to remember to send someone over there in a day or two to let them know about Fred.

Greyson Leigh certainly shouldn't set foot in that place for a year, not if his first appearance had ended up with Jansen in the hospital. The locals wouldn't find that nearly as unfortunate and he'd probably end up shooting someone before he could get back out the door safely.

Let Parsons send a uniformed officer around to tell them.

But not until after Greyson Leigh had what he needed.

"What are we looking for?" Rachel asked, stepping close to that vanity where the computer rested but not turning the machine on.

Greyson joined her. Most people tended to leave their lives on their personal machines. Certainly, the work comm was always subject to all manner of rules and restrictions about what you could do with it.

Plus Internal Affairs routinely inspected them from the back side.

The rules weren't enforced that much, because Hunters tended to also have to meander into the darker corners of cyberspace as well as the streets when they were at work, but still…

Greyson wondered if there was a way to have someone in Computer Forensics take this machine apart for him without making too big of a noise back at the Bureau. Did anyone owe him favors? Or hate Jansen enough?

Closer now, he saw something interesting out of the corner of his eye. Greyson reached out a hand and flipped on the light switch. Half the bulbs didn't come on, but they were perfect even/odd, so he presumed that Jansen had set them that way.

All the lights on and it would be too bright to do anything but apply makeup.

Jansen had pictures tucked into the frames of the mirror. Actual photographs on paper. Weird. Lots of them, all the way around, showing the life you'd never guess a guy like Fred had indulged in.

Sporting events. Concerts. Cars.

Huh.

When Greyson had been a kid, nobody did that, but that was him showing his age. Up until the last bits of the Twentieth Century, everything was done with chemical film. Then electronic cameras came along and everyone just recorded images.

At one point, various social media sites had come along in cyberspace and you uploaded them all for the world to look at, but folks tended to take thousands of shots and then forget about them until their comm was full and they had to either offload them to be lost forever or delete a bunch.

Ink printed on paper almost represented an archaeological thing. He felt like he should bring a research librarian in here just so he could have them explain what that generation before he'd been born had been like, except he was familiar enough with it to tell Rachel if he needed.

Jansen wasn't that old. The man was thirty-seven. Average as cops went. Young for humans, as he hadn't even reached that middle-aged stretch where you had a mid-life crisis.

But law enforcement tended to chew people up, so you could qualify for a full pension at twenty years, depending. The army had been the same way, and Greyson had that money land in his account every month, two days before his paycheck.

He wondered if Jansen might be close enough to qualify for a medical hardship when he got out of the hospital, if he ended up getting caught up in whatever conspiracy Greyson found.

Might be a good way for Parsons or Upkins to get the man out of the way politely.

Because there was a second picture kind of tucked behind what looked like a concert ticket for a band Greyson had never heard of, playing a show downtown six years ago.

Greyson pulled the one from behind. The one that had caught his eye even though he couldn't initially tell what it was.

Maybe the placement had looked guilty? Tuck it in out of sight from a casual stranger breaking into the place, like Greyson and Rachel, but still at hand? Something.

And important enough to have been printed, saved, and displayed on the mirror where Fred Jansen did all his work.

Greyson didn't recognize the boat, but he knew where the picture had been taken. And the two men in it, posing in front of a big fish hanging mouth-down from a scale on a wharf. In a marina with perfect sun and amazingly blue water.

Fred Jansen, with one arm around Olek Jan Zielinski's shoulders, both men smiling like fiends.

"Oh," Rachel spoke up from close enough that he could smell her shampoo. "Florida, huh? That's our next stop?"

"Florida," Greyson nodded.

Zielinski had retired down there as the price of Greyson Leigh coming back into harness. But the tan on the man's face said that this picture wasn't all that old.

Maybe a month or two? Right after someone had stolen a picture from a computer file? And knew a place where you could get them printed out on real, honest to goodness paper as a personal memento?

Greyson wondered if Zielinski had told the man at the time that it was going to be a target on a dartboard or something equally bland and innocent.

Or if Fred Jansen had already been in it up to his nose when Greyson walked into that bar to ask.

He was going to need some answers soon.

[16]

DOWNTOWN

Rachel could tell, just from the set of his shoulders as they walked back to the car with a duffle bag full of clothes for Jansen when he got released, that Greyson was going to cause trouble. The nasty kind.

She'd never seen the grief between the man and Zielinski, but Greyson had been gone before she arrived. In fact, near as she could tell, she'd permanently filled the slot in the department that had opened when Greyson Leigh got forcibly retired the first time.

But she'd been partnered with the notorious playboy Carlos Dominguez for those long months. Not a stone-cold killer like Leigh.

And then Zielinski had been the price Greyson demanded of the Metropolitan for his return.

Gone, just like that. But she knew now that nobody but Leigh could have solved that case. Those two Phrenic had been too lucky.

Sure, they were smart. The species had been engineered for brains and social capability. You needed that to be able to shapeshift into someone else and fool their closest friends and lovers. Having access to their memories was good, but only got you so far.

And the more she learned, the more Rachel understood that Greyson Leigh had just been the blunt instrument that the Metropolitan had been wanting to use to clean up the Boston office of the Bureau, without all the secondary scandals that might have come out and destroyed lives.

Too much blackmail on the table. Or under it.

Had Captain Zielinski understood that he had a chance to walk away clean? There had always been the presumption that nobody would bother the man if he retired down to Florida or wherever ex-cops and Hunters went when they stopped doing the job.

Or had he needed this long to set all this scam up in a way that probably would have worked, had that first event ended with Greyson and maybe her both dead in that square?

The night was cold as they walked, and she wasn't warming up keeping up with Greyson's long legs. Probably should have grabbed the heavier jacket from the hook after her shower, but she'd been distracted by getting her new body armor to sit comfortably.

She'd taken Greyson's advice and upgraded. He still didn't have anything but cotton between him and death, but he didn't give two shits if he lived or died and Rachel wasn't sure what it would take to break the man out of his depression.

Did Greyson even know he was exhibiting clinical symptoms? Probably not. The man had never done higher education beyond public high school. And the army wouldn't have given him the tools to self-diagnose.

Too much risk that he'd realize he was likely to be dead before he was twenty-eight, and either stop being an effective operative, or turn into a suicidal maniac in the field.

Somehow, he'd lived this long, nearly fifty, and was still

going like hell. Was it luck or just stubbornness on his part? Maybe some combination.

She'd researched Phrenic. And had access to all sorts of information about the species that was never made public.

They killed their target and then used those face tentacles to slip into their eye sockets and pretty much suck out the interesting bits of their brain chemistry, overlaying it onto their own so that they could impersonate someone physically as well as socially. They could only have one set of characteristics at a time, but frequently killed several bodies and drained them into husks, where they could go back and get enough taste to rotate between people.

Or so the aliens explained it.

That one book had described Phrenic as using a mental projection of their victim, like a standing hologram between them and the outside world, letting that projection handle everything.

Sometimes, something went wrong.

Deathwalker was the term used to describe a Phrenic that had lost control of the projection of their victim. Supposedly, they reverted to base form Phrenic: scales, chitin, and tentacles; but with the victim's personality in control, so just exactly the opposite of the normal routine. Didn't last long, because a human or some other species had no idea how to handle the situation and ended up jumping off a ledge or otherwise offing themselves.

Rachel Asher had no way to prove it short of going there, but Greyson had given her all the clues she needed, to assume that he had been killed by a second Phrenic and impersonated. It made a twisted bit of perfect sense, after they had failed to get Dominguez's brain when Rachel herself stopped the creature over Carlos's dead body.

Who would be the next person the Hunter Bureau would call?

The very best killer of all time, except that he was retired. Forced out of the Bureau and living as a civilian.

Who might not even realize that he was a target. At least not until someone came in the window, late at night, and killed him.

Stupid bastard had gotten more than he bargained for, though.

Greyson Leigh. Toughest son of a bitch in New England, to hear the old salts talk.

Somehow, the Phrenic had lost control, and Greyson had taken over their body, without losing everything. Had the Phrenic just given up? According to the books she'd snuck in —home alone without Greyson anywhere nearby to read— the combined body was supposed to just die.

She could see Leigh forcing it to survive.

How long did he have?

Phrenic were a long-lived species, so maybe longer than Greyson's normal lifespan?

He caught her staring and was about to ask when his comm chirped in a pocket. They were almost to the car, so he grabbed the keys with one hand and the comm with the other.

Greyson tossed the keyring to her as he answered, so she grabbed the duffle bag from him as well and walked the last twenty meters to the Skycruiser and popped the back door open.

Greyson was having a cop conversation with someone. All monosyllables at this end. She stood close at hand and started to keep watch, but he hung up quickly and turned to her.

"Quick stop before we return to the hospital," he said cryptically. "You drive."

And just like that, he turned and walked to the car,

except that he went around to the passenger side and looked at her expectantly.

Rachel shrugged and got in.

"Where are we going?" she asked as she moved the damned seat up to where normal people, the ones that weren't all leg, could drive. And adjusted all the mirrors. And the steering wheel.

With grumbles that only got worse as she caught his grin out of the corner of her eye.

"Downtown," he said. "To talk to Quinton Laux. He says he has something for us."

"Am I going to like it?" she asked.

"Probably not," he grinned some more. "But if you'd wanted a boring job, you could have stayed a cop."

Rachel grumbled some more.

Damn it, she hated when he was right.

[17]

LATENCY

GREYSON HAD NEEDED HER TO DRIVE SO HE COULD look some things up. It wasn't that he didn't trust the car to drive itself. He didn't trust all the other idiots out there that wouldn't let the car controls handle themselves.

Laux had used a specific term and Greyson didn't understand all the implications. So Rachel was dealing with people out late or up early as the sun was getting ready to come up soon.

Latency.

According to the cybernauts who thought important things and posted them for the world to see, the word had two main meanings.

First: *the delay before a transfer of data begins following the instructions for the transfer.*

Second: *the state of existing but not yet being developed or manifest. Aka Concealment.*

Greyson was familiar with the second from criminal investigations. Latent prints were invisible until you dusted and extracted them from a door handle or refrigerator. Great way to prove a perp had been at the scene of a crime, but not generally sufficient to convict, in and of themselves.

And Greyson also remembered being a kid playing computer games, where lag equaled death in the first person shooters that had been popular in those days. Your avatar could not react fast enough to shoot someone else, especially if he had a lower latency and could shoot you first.

Why had Laux said he had a question about latency? Odd term for a civilian to use. But this was an odd case.

He let Rachel drive and grumble quietly while he ruminated like a cow with particularly good cud.

The parking garage was open. There was a twenty-four-hour grocery up on the ground floor. The kind that would validate his parking if he cared enough to go up and buy something. Three bucks wasn't going to break the bank, or probably even be enough to justify turning in an expense report for reimbursement.

They circled all the way down and parked, like before. Walked back up a level and got into that elevator.

Greyson was surprised that there were no indigents or drunks back here, but he supposed that Laux had ways of chivying them on their way.

Hopefully, it was just annoying and not particularly dangerous.

Into the elevator and down. Out into that big room.

Laux had the side door already open by the time they got there.

The man was in a nicer suit this time. Not quite what Greyson would have worn for a night out with Emmy, but close. Single-breasted in the Western style. Three buttons all undone to sit. Nice silk tie. He led Greyson and Rachel down to the same office as before.

"Thanks for coming," Laux said simply as they sat.

"Worried about the time, but figured that you might still be awake now, and that calling in six hours would be the rude choice."

"Close enough," Greyson replied. "We were working and just about to call it a morning. We're here. How can I help?"

"Maybe I can help you," Laux said.

"Latency," Greyson offered.

"I think I know how to make your Synth Chip work," Laux said simply. "How to get someone to believe they are in a visual fantasy land that is so much more realistic than anything they've ever imagined possible in such a chip."

"Aren't they realistic already?" Rachel spoke up.

Greyson would have asked the same question, but he hadn't moved as fast.

"No," Laux said simply. "Yes, the visuals are stunning. And you get sound and smells as well on the good ones. Touch is easy to simulate, because you're supposed to just cut out all that circuitry and route it through the chip. But anyone plugged to a Synth Chip never loses the fact that they are in a simulation. The amount of processing power necessary to handle every one of those little details is still more than anything you could get except from being inside one of the alien's astrogation computers."

"Why?" Greyson asked bluntly. "Most of that sensory information is never processed by the mind."

"Correct," Laux nodded, looking and sounding more and more like a professor.

Greyson had wondered about the man's background, but wasn't about to pry.

"However, while the active mind doesn't do anything with all that data, the brain still has to process it," Laux continued. "In the real world, everything just gets shunted off and dropped. People like Detectives usually have a secondary mental thread sniffing through it all, and that lets them pick up those subtle hints and clues."

"But the Synth Chip doesn't bother with all that," Rachel extended the thought. "So you have an unconscious understanding that none of that is real."

"Yes," Laux said. "I'm willing to bet that someone built filters into that chip of yours to make sure that your shooter didn't get as much sensory data as they should, specifically to trick them into thinking that they were in a sim."

"Latency," Greyson said. "Artificial in this case. What other things could you do?"

"That's what frightens me, Leigh," the man continued. "He was inside a high-end Synth that convinced him he was just seated on his couch at home, doing things to imaginary people that he would probably never do in the real world. I was having dinner with some friends, talking in very vague and general terms about the technology itself, rather than the specifics of this case, when I had a very interesting idea. Without access to the chip itself, I can't prove it, but I have a theory I would like to run past you. It goes beyond latency."

"Beyond?" Rachel asked, still a little confused, but unwilling to start looking things up, like Greyson had done on the way over there.

Or: why Rachel got to drive tonight instead of him.

"*Beyond*," Laux agreed, adding extra emphasis on the word.

"Talk to me," Greyson said. "Can't promise anything, but I have connections I could ask, if I thought it was worth it."

"Reality is perception," Laux said. "A number of important philosophers have argued the topic for centuries."

"Sure," Rachel said. "The brain in the vat theory."

Greyson had no idea what she was talking about, but she was the one getting a college degree. He was just a killer in a nice shirt that Emmy had bought him.

"So what happens when you can be just a brain in a vat, Detectives?" Laux asked. "When perhaps the technological advances are sufficient that I can substitute my reality for yours?"

"Shit," Rachel whispered in a tiny voice, like a six-year-old that has had a nightmare and wasn't getting the reassurances she wanted. The ones that said the monsters under the bed aren't real.

"Yeah," Laux agreed. "So suppose now that I can drop enough of that sensory input to make you think you are in a Synth, but then I don't? Maybe I just alter how you hear and smell and see things to make the world around you almost the same, but not quite? You become a brain in my vat, but that's expensive to maintain for very long."

"How would you get around it?" Greyson asked.

"I'd upload something that might be otherwise classified as a computer virus, except that I'm doing it directly to your brain," the man pronounced. "Burn out a few places. Add a couple of cross-wires that nature never intended. Insert some false memories in places nobody would ever expect. Mind you, in my line of work we specifically avoid doing that."

"Why's that?" Greyson asked.

"Bad for business, man," the professor smiled with perfect teeth showing bright against his dark skin. "I live on repeat customers. Can't get that if I'm killing people or burning out their minds. That's why Synth Chips are so tightly regulated. We don't push those edges. Instead, we provide certain fantasies that more vanilla folks in authority might not be willing to allow for the citizenry. Content, rather than medium."

"But you think that the chip had to burn out pieces of the shooter's mind in order to work?" Greyson pressed.

"Can't see any other way to do it," Laux replied, sobering.

"And I'm as good as anybody you're likely to find in this field. Better than most, too."

Greyson considered the man. Liz thought highly enough of him, and his ethics, to recommend that they meet. That went a long ways with Greyson.

"Can you get me a map of the damage you think they'd have to do?" Greyson asked. "The places and the outcomes?"

"Why?" Laux leaned back now, more wary.

"Because I can ask the coroner for a briefing and compare your notes to hers," Greyson smiled grimly. "If you're on to something, then I can go to my Captain and the Metropolitan herself, and ask for them to let me share some of the more intimate details with you. Rachel and I are pursuing a different aspect of the case, but I'm just trying to take down the mastermind behind it all. Your help might be necessary to unravel how they did it and stop them from doing it again?"

"Truly?" the man asked, shocked now. "But I'm a criminal, Detective Leigh."

"No," Greyson countered with a smile. "You are an expert civilian that I have engaged as a consultant on technical aspects of this case that I could not have understood otherwise. If they have a bitch with that, they can take it up with me, not you."

Laux studied him for a long moment.

"There are pieces of this that you aren't telling me," he said.

"Oh, that I can promise you," Greyson smiled. "But none of it is likely to circle back and bite you on the ass. Get me the bits I need to convince them that you're on the level and maybe I can tell you more."

He rose now and shook the man's hand. Quinton Laux had given him the piece he needed.

No law-abiding fab had done the work. Could do the

work. And whoever had built that chip had to have probably known that they would have to destroy the victim's mind to make it work.

That made it murder in the first degree.

After he got back from Florida, he'd be setting off after them next.

[18]

BULLET

GREYSON NAVIGATED EARLY MORNING TRAFFIC AND LET Rachel ride in quiet. He was up to no good, but she was taking it all in stride.

The first thing the aliens had done when they made themselves known to Earthlings had been to upgrade the transportation networks.

Greyson had approved then and really appreciated them now.

Superfast trains had already worked in other countries because the governments had been able to get right of way. In the old United States, NIMBY had delayed everything for so long that it was never economical to actually build.

Not In My Back Yard.

Then the middle-class bastards had the audacity to complain about bad roads and crowded airports after preventing every other possible fix in the name of sticking it to someone else instead. Not that he had any strong opinions on the topic or anything.

The Illymus Merchant Guild had brought in bullet trains of a different sort. And cheated in North America.

Greyson liked sticking it back hard to those NIMBY people.

The power lines already ran everywhere. Alien tech had been able to string an extra line on top of those poles and harden it into a beam. Run a pulsating current through it to keep the birds from settling, and you had a rail corridor one to two hundred feet in the air, silent except for the wind of a train shooting by at five hundred kilometers per hour.

They only stopped at major cities to keep the throughput high. From Boston, you could go directly north to several Canadian cities, like Montréal, Québec City, and Halifax. Southwards you hit New York, Philly, and then DC, skipping places like New Haven or Baltimore, but being able to catch a local train that was slower, but still faster than anything they'd had in this country when he was a kid.

The key was not stopping at every little podunk to take on passengers. Or hostages, depending on how you wanted to see things.

"Where *are* we going?" Rachel finally asked in a voice that didn't really expect any sort of answer she would like, but felt resigned to actually asking anyway.

But hey, she was still his partner. She should have known better by now.

Greyson grinned over at the woman.

"You've had a shower and got on clean clothes," he replied in that false brightness guaranteed to instigate an extra heavy eyeroll as the sun was considering coming up soon.

"You're not even going to tell them, are you?" she fired back, having already done the math and drawn the right conclusion.

"Not telling anyone, kid," he said fiercely as he turned off the street and into a long-term parking lot.

In a day or two, he might call the car on his comm and

tell it to return to the Bureau lot. Or he might leave it here to get him home when he got back.

"There's paperwork we're supposed to fill out first," Rachel reminded him as he found a spot and pulled in.

"We're in hot pursuit," he grinned. "Besides, if I ask for permission, someone will leak it and our target will disappear. Cuba's not that far away, and, in spite of everyone being friendly neighbors these days, they still don't really like *Los Anglos del Norte*, or even *Puerto Ricans*. They can make my life hell until I bring enough firepower to the table."

"And that would rob you of the chance to do this personally, wouldn't it?" she fired back as she opened the door.

"You got it."

He joined her and they started walking to the light rail station that would haul them a couple of miles to the bullet terminal. Again, if you were looking at his geocodes on a screen, nothing that would stand out and suggest you call your buddy in Florida and let him know that trouble was coming.

Just a quick jaunt. Hop a bullet and be there in time for dinner.

And not leave a trail at the airport, which was where everyone would probably look for him, if they realized he was about to pull this sort of stunt.

They got up onto the platform and the next car was about five minutes away. The rest of the people waiting around them were either the last dregs of the party hounds headed home, the immigrant women and men who cleaned offices at night, or the folks headed somewhere early before going into the office. A gym, maybe, or a non-neighborhood coffee shop where they met up with friends to shoot the shit before the day started.

He and Rachel didn't really stand out that much. She'd had a shower a few hours ago and he was good enough.

Plus, Greyson was planning to get a cabin on the train, with a private bathroom and beds, so he could shower, sleep, and eat out of the dining car as they traveled, more or less anonymously.

You'll never see me coming.

[19]

SOUTHBOUND

Rachel surveyed the accommodations with jaundiced eye, following the conductor who took them up to the second floor of the car and showed them the room Greyson had apparently reserved when she wasn't looking.

Private, but she didn't think he was up to no good. Even if she'd been interested in a romp with a dry, sarcastic punk like Leigh. Which she generally wasn't.

"And you have two sofas facing each other," the man was explaining. "They can be pulled out for sleeping on long trips, forming a queen-sized bed. This is your private bathroom, with a shower and toilet. The dining car is the next car rear of you. Upstairs is a full kitchen and usually a waiting list. Downstairs looks more like a coffee shop, but they have a hotplate. Think hotdog stand with a few more options, but personally I find Xi to be a better cook than the fancy people. Is there anything else I can get you?"

"We're good," Greyson spoke up. "Been up all night, so I might just crash on the couch for now and then grab some breakfast when we hit Manhattan."

Rachel watching him slide the guy a meafle, the ten loonie note with the maple leaf on the front, and got a tip of an invisible cap in return.

"Please let me know," he said. "My cabin is across and forward, just next to the stairs."

And then he was gone, leaving the two lovebirds alone. Or the old fart running off with his *chica*?

Rachel wondered how the conductor might have rated them, without knowing anything except that they were dressed pretty nice, had been up all night, and didn't have any luggage.

How many people suddenly eloped on a train like this? Not like old Las Vegas was involved. It didn't have the panache it used to, but was still a place for middle-class office drones to vacation, with just enough carefully-curated seediness to give you a thrill.

If you had real money, you probably jet-setted to some private island. If you were poor, there were still tribal casinos scattered around that would take your money for an evening's entertainment.

Rachel hadn't even packed her bikini.

But then, she doubted that she'd have need for it, unless Greyson wanted to distract someone with her ass while he was breaking in somewhere. Except that maybe she'd put him in a speedo and let the old ladies hit on poor Greyson while she got out the lockpicks.

Turnabout, my friend.

But she just smiled and studied the exhaustion etched into his face with a chisel.

"Food or sleep first?" she asked as he stood there, a little blank.

"Sleep," he finally said. "Wake me when they announce New York City and we'll grab some food before all those folks board. Most of them are headed to DC for work, so they'll be after coffee and bagels."

"Commuting?" Rachel asked, a little staggered.

"Not that much longer of a trip on the bullet than it used to be driving in from the suburbs when I was a kid, Rachel," he countered in a serious voice. "Probably spend longer driving to the station and parking than you do in flight."

"Weird," she decided.

"Agreed," he said. "But remember that everyone has their own calculations to make about how they want to do things. The world—hell the whole galaxy—is much smaller than it was thirty years ago, let alone a hundred or a thousand. We're making a run to Florida today, and not even flying or taking the sub-orbital."

She shrugged. Sneaking up on that bastard is what they were doing, but she wasn't about to say that out loud. They were in public and someone might draw the wrong conclusion.

She closed the door and watched Greyson kick off his shoes and put his jacket and holsters on the floor where he could get at them quickly if he needed to.

"I need some coffee," she told him.

He nodded and stretched out on the right-hand sofa, then got up and located a blanket in a pantry she hadn't seen before. Like this wasn't his first rodeo, or something.

But the man was going to be fifty this year. Twenty-seven years older than her. What other crazy shit had he done in his time? How much of it would ever come out?

And if he really was an alien wearing Greyson Leigh's skin, how much of that knowledge could she tap?

Rachel knew that she was supposed to turn him in on suspicion, wherein they would probably have to nerve scramble him to take him down if he really was a Phrenic, with that second nervous system they had. Then he'd be dead.

Depending on how paranoid they were, she'd be put to the question pretty hard after that. At best, she'd turn into a laughingstock, to have not noticed that her partner had been taken over.

Except that she'd never met the real Greyson Leigh. It had happened before he came back.

If that same one that got Dominguez got Leigh a few days later, she'd always been partnered with an infiltrator. And a damned good cop and Hunter, from everything he had been at pains to teach her over the last six months.

Like maybe he was doing penance.

Rachel let herself out and headed rear and down, nodding mutely at other passengers as they boarded and got settled.

She needed time to plan. She'd only had Zielinski as a boss for eight months before he was out. Might and might not remember her, except that he'd set Greyson up, so he probably had her picture somewhere handy. Maybe as a target in whatever shooting range he belonged to.

Hopefully not for less prurient reasons.

Ick.

At least Greyson was always a gentleman. And had Emmy to handle his needs.

She got in line for coffee, eventually ordering a mocha instead an Americano. Rachel figured she needed the sugar and fat today. She was going to be burning energy at a high rate.

Her comm chirped with a message as she got her cup and looked for a spot to quietly sit and sip.

Most of the folks in there had that look of commuters, now that Greyson had pointed it out to her.

Live in Boston, work in Manhattan? I suppose if you're in

*finance or the like and don't want to deal with a helicopter or
flitter from the Hamptons or Montauk.*

Rachel shrugged and pulled her comm out.

Train? - Redhawk.

She wondered what system had been monitoring for
signs of her and Greyson doing things like leaving town. The
six North American Metropolitans were, in some ways, even
more powerful as politicians than the President of the United
States, since that one was mostly a ceremonial role these days.

The Eastern Metroplex itself combined Boston, New
York, and DC, but the region Upkins controlled was huge.
Panama City, Florida was just inside the Eastern Region,
rather than the Southern, based out of Houston and
including much of the middle of the country.

"Yup," she typed back, sipping at the mocha and sending
negative waves at any of the suits around her that might
think she looked cute and single.

She was, but not the least bit interested in these schmos.

Destination?

Rachel laughed. If their system had noticed her and
Greyson buying tickets, or him buying a double with a cabin,
then Redhawk already knew where they were going. Given
the three primary suspects right now, it narrowed things
remarkably well.

"Fishing," Rachel sent back, harking back to that picture
of Fred and Zielinski in front of some critter they had
apparently pulled from the depths.

Backup?

"That would be me," she typed, scowling at a stock
broker type in a fancy suit eyeing her from across the way.

She wondered if she should just flash her badge at the
guy, or if that sort of thing might act like an aphrodisiac on
men like him.

They all seemed to want bimbos or the forbidden.

And pumpkin over there seemed to spend more time on his mascara game every morning than Rachel's mom did. Granted, he got better results, but that wasn't saying much.

She decided that maybe what she needed was one of those lumberjack types that women always ran into when they went home for the holidays, at least in the books and vids she consumed.

The kind of guy whose idea of 'scaping anything involved a machete and an ax.

Keep me posted. Leigh never will.

She laughed out loud at that, wondering just how well Edgar Redhawk knew her partner to be able to confidently assume that up front.

It wasn't that he was wrong, mind you. But that he already knew what was coming.

That spoke of some enormous battles for information in the past.

Not that Greyson Leigh was the only person Rachel knew who might possibly be more stubborn than she was. Perish the thought.

"Will try," Rachel sent and then stuffed the comm back into her pocket.

Pretty boy over there apparently took that as a sign, as he rose to walk over and shower her with his awesome masculinity.

Or something equally lame.

Rachel rose and stepped right up to him, fishing in her inner jacket pocket for her badge.

She flipped it open in his face and sniffed really loudly.

He staggered back a half step in surprise.

"No, you appear human," she announced loud enough that everyone in the car without headphones in could hear her. "Rumors of an alien infiltration. Have a good day, citizen."

Rachel slipped around the paralyzed man, trying not to giggle out loud as she went up the stairs and then crossed forward to her car.

Technically, she might even be right about aliens being aboard, but she might have pulled something like that on the pretty punk in the expensive suit anyway.

She had more important game to pursue.

[20]

DREAMER

GREYSON SLEPT.

At least he thought so. Some nights it was hard to tell where dreaming ended and waking nightmares became truth. He'd been up for twenty-something hours at this point.

A door opened in his mind and a creature stepped out of the closet into the hallway, scowling angrily at him.

Biped. Monster covered over with scales and such like a leatherback turtle. As Greyson watched, the face began to shift. Morph. Transform into someone familiar.

Greyson Leigh stared back at him a moment later. In dream logic, the man was even wearing the same gray slacks and white shirt.

Ethen.

The Phrenic who had killed him originally. Who had used a projection of Greyson Leigh, based on personality and memories, to fool everyone into believing that Greyson Leigh still existed.

Right up to the point that Zaborra had shot him—them —with a nerve scrambler. It should have killed them.

Except that Greyson Leigh was too stubborn to die, even when he was only a ghost in another man's mind.

"I can save us," Greyson, the ghost Greyson, had said in that moment. "But you have to let me. You have to let go, Ethen."

Ethen had dreamed of Deathwalkers. Phrenic that had lost control of that mind and let the ghost take over, until they failed and died.

"No," Greyson had reminded the creature. "I can't survive without you. But you won't live without me. Let go, and I can save us from Zaborra. I can save Rachel, and you'll get all the credit."

"You will," Ethen had tried to say even as his mind—their mind—was shutting down. "I'm pretending to be you, because you're a better man than I am."

"Today, perhaps," Greyson had said. "Tomorrow is your chance to change that. Just let go, Ethen."

And Ethen had let go that night. Greyson had been in charge of their body since. But even frightened Ethen would surface occasionally to haunt his dreams.

Usually when the stress was reaching dangerous levels.

"Rachel suspects," Ethen said, wearing his face like a funhouse mirror.

"Rachel knows," Greyson replied unequivocally.

"Why hasn't she killed us?" Ethen asked.

Greyson shrugged in response. Ethen existed inside his mind. Or he inside Ethen's.

The Phrenic infiltrator could see all the reasons Greyson had chalked up on a board as notes.

"She believes me," Greyson told his ghost. "She understands that we're going to make her a better cop than I ever was."

"And when she is?" Ethen asked. "When she no longer needs us?"

"Maybe she kills us, Ethen," Greyson replied. "Maybe she sends us off to kill ourselves in such a way that nobody ever knows what happened. Maybe she tells you to kill someone else and take their life, hoping that maybe you'll be happier."

"I'd rather die than take another life, Greyson," the man moaned. "You were the last. When she's done then I'm done."

"There you go," Greyson said simply. "We live until we can't do any more good in the world. But we'll have done good. We will leave this world a better place than we found it."

Greyson watched the other man morph through a dozen faces in as many seconds, standing in what appeared to be Greyson's kitchenette now, back in that one place both of them felt safe. Man, woman. Human, alien.

Then he turned back into a base form Phrenic again, the hairless thing with scutes and scales. A blank face with big eyes and almost no nose.

"I just want to sleep," Ethen said in a sad voice.

"You rest," Greyson assured him. "I'll watch over us like I always do. You'll be safe."

Ethen turned and walked to a door that didn't exist in the real world, opening it and stepping into a dark closet where he could pull the door shut and hide from all the things he had done in a life of junior varsity crime.

Greyson would have liked to have found a way to raise Zaborra from the dead, just so he could kill that son of a bitch a few more times for what he'd done to Ethen when they were partners.

Ethen was a follower. Always had been. Zaborra had been the bully who did all the gaslighting. Who had twisted a weak person like Ethen into a follower. A victim.

Made him kill people and take all the risk, so that

Zaborra didn't have to, but could still live a life of crime and debauchery.

Who knew how long they would have gone on, had Zaborra not decided to try his luck with the primitive monkeys on Earth? How much damage might they have done if they hadn't gone after the Hunter Bureau directly, with some stupid scheme to hide behind the face of the Hunters sent to catch them.

But Zaborra was dead. Never coming back. Greyson had killed him using Ethen's hand and Greyson's gun.

Ethen could rest now.

Greyson would protect him, just like he did all the other innocents.

In the end, that's what Hunters did.

[21]

STALKING THE ELUSIVE PREY

GREYSON OPENED HIS EYES AND CHECKED THE TIME ON his comm before he realized that Rachel was seated across from him, quietly reading and drinking coffee from a paper cup.

He'd been down for an hour. Felt like ten seconds. Or ten days.

"I was about three minutes from waking you up for Manhattan," she announced in a quiet voice. "You were having a pretty bad nightmare when I got back, but then you settled, so I started reading and let you just breathe."

Greyson sat up and rubbed his eyes. The conductor had left the curtains closed originally, so it was dim in here. That was good. He grabbed his holsters and started reassembling his mind and body, thinking about the coffee Rachel had.

His stomach woke up and complained.

"Thank you for letting me sleep," he said as he reached for his shoes. "I needed that. You'll need downtime before we arrive."

"Caffeine burns out of my system pretty quick," she

grinned at him and put her reader away. "Should we head aft and get some food?"

"Yeah," he muttered, standing and stretching.

It felt like he'd been beaten with canes while he slept, but that was just the nightmare thing.

Other people might drink to drown those sorrows, but Greyson was made of sterner stuff. He'd abide.

They rose and Rachel smiled up at him. Friendly.

Greyson wondered if her face would break doing that, as sad as it seemed to him. He'd thought his own might, a time or two.

But he returned the smile. It seemed to lift something off his shoulders.

They got to the cafe upstairs just as a rush of people were leaving, apparently getting off at Manhattan.

The manager took a look at the two of them, smiled, and seated them in a weird corner where a section of wall cut into the booth.

Space for two, where most of the others in here were for four or maybe six, depending. Last time he'd ridden a train like this, they just randomly seated you with strangers based on time or reservation.

Hell, did the man think they were lovebirds? Seated alone where they could whisper sweet nothings to each other across the table and maybe hold hands?

Greyson tried not to roll his eyes.

The waitress was a pro. Came quick. Got orders for coffee and left menus. Retreated around the corner into the kitchen space. Left them alone.

Rachel pulled out her comm and spun it around so he could read the screen. She powered it on and opened the texting app to a conversation with…

Edgar Redhawk?

Interesting.

Greyson wasn't all that surprised. Except that maybe they were watching him closer than he had expected.

Greyson had originally figured that the call would come about the time they hit Richmond. Or maybe as late as Raleigh when neither of them came into the office or checked in by noon.

For a long moment, he wondered if he should ask Quinton Laux about setting up a fake credit account for him under some other name, just so he could hide and not be tracked through the system electronically.

Make people like Parsons and Redhawk work a little harder to keep tabs on him.

But it was a momentary itch he could ignore.

As long as it didn't become a habit on their part to follow him wherever he went. That might just piss him off.

"I done good?" Rachel asked as he handed her back the device.

"You did," Greyson told her, remembering that for all her skill and ruthlessness, Rachel Asher was still only twenty-three. Wet behind the ears in a lot of ways, but getting better. "I'd like to show up on the man's doorstep unannounced, if that's still possible. I have no idea who might leak, but I doubt that Redhawk is a threat. That man exists to protect Denise from people like Zielinski."

"Probably sees us as his hunting dogs?" she asked.

"As good a comparison as any," he nodded.

He ordered a heavy breakfast, assuming a long day and not many options once they got to Panama City. Once Zielinski knew they were there, all hell would probably break loose.

"So are we just knocking on his door to give the man a heart attack, or do we have a plan when we get there?" Rachel asked after they were alone again.

"Considered a number of options," Greyson replied as a placeholder.

"I didn't bring a bikini, so you'd have to take me shopping if we go down that path," she retorted with a grin.

He couldn't tell how serious she was. She didn't do flirtatious with him all that much, but it slipped out occasionally. Like she was doing right now.

But she also read Cop/Alien romance books, so he had to walk a fine line, unwilling to ask exactly where the woman's kinks might run to.

"Doubt you'd manage to turn Zielinski's head," Greyson said in a more serious tone. "Never once saw him show any interest in anybody that way, male or female. Man might be an ace, for all I know."

Ace. Slang term for someone exhibiting Asexual tendencies. Greyson was just old enough to remember the great awakening in this culture, when everyone discovered that there were more options than white-bread hetero.

Folks like that had always been there, but for the longest time the power structure in his country had come down hard on anyone deviating from the strict party line, both legally as well as socially.

Greyson just assumed that Zielinski hated everyone too much to want to fuck them.

His own anger probably kept him warm at night. Greyson had known a few people like that over the years.

Rachel grinned at some internal joke and shrugged.

"So inviting him to dinner probably doesn't get you the results you want," she continued. "Unless scaring the man shitless is the purpose of this trip."

It was Greyson's turn to grin. There was something to be said for it.

He owed Olek a few, going back more than a decade. This might be his last chance to cash those tokens in.

"We're way ahead of anything that man had planned," Greyson replied. "First off, we survived. Second, we're on this case. Third, it's only been about twelve hours since Jansen got run over, so Zielinski might not even know that something happened, let alone our connection to it."

"What if he's not there?" she asked.

Greyson felt a mental earthquake nearly knock him out of the booth. He'd been assuming he could just show up and hustle the man, push him, knock him sideways into enough of a confession to bring in warrants and Forensics folks after he arrested Zielinski on suspicion of a crime for long enough that he couldn't destroy any evidence.

What if they did this and Zielinski wasn't there?

Or better, what if they could draw him out of his lair?

"I like you, kid," Greyson said, the two of them grinning.

"Call Redhawk and have someone pass a message along to Zielinski that Jansen got hurt?" she asked. "If Jansen's in a coma for a few days, he can't spill anything good to Zielinski right away. Gives us time to commit another Breaking and Entering. And we're in our jurisdiction, however barely."

"Yeah," Greyson nearly growled. "We'll make the call about the time we hit Jacksonville. That's mid-afternoon. Maybe time for him to drop everything and jump on a plane or semi-ballistic back to Boston and not clean things up here."

"He got a dog?" she asked.

"Doubt it," Greyson said. "That would be someone he had to care for. Take care of. Maybe even like. Don't see him ever being that friendly to any creature."

"So we can possibly get in without being seen," Rachel said. "Assuming he doesn't have any hookers tied up or anything. Then what?"

"People live messy lives when they aren't expecting Hunters to show up," Greyson said. "Fred had that picture. It was innocent enough, except that it tied the two men together in time and place in a way that made Fred look really bad. Zielinski doesn't come out of that looking much better."

"Yeah, the Captain I remember wasn't that geeky," Rachel pivoted the conversation on him. "Where'd he get that chip made? I can see the gun. Bunch of cops and Hunters seem to have that fetish."

"Maybe we'll get lucky and the man got a receipt for it," Greyson said.

"But we're really going to take him down?" Rachel asked.

"If the man gives me any reason to, Rachel," Greyson said. "Somebody wanted you and me dead. Don't forget that part. I'm guessing it was Zielinski, but if not, I'll apologize to the man in my head and we'll start looking at Kwan and Owens next."

She nodded and fell silent as food arrived.

Greyson didn't figure he'd ever have to say he was sorry. Not with a punk like Olek Zielinski.

[22]

JACKSONVILLE

THEY HAD BLASTED THROUGH THE SOUTHERN PORTION of the Atlantic seaboard from Raleigh without any incident, other than Rachel taking her turn to have a quick nap while Greyson watched over her.

He had picked this train because it skipped Atlanta and all that craziness, although you could exit here in Jacksonville and take a spoke line inland, on the way to Memphis and then either Chicago or Dallas, depending.

The rest of the day had passed easily enough. Outside, it was mid-afternoon, but you could never tell.

It was raining like hell as the train pulled to a stop and people started migrating. Pissing hard rain so bad that you could barely see the terminal building below.

Helped Greyson feel like he was sneaking up on his prey.

Rachel sat across from him and read, looking up now as he double-checked that the cabin door was shut and pulled his comm. Edgar Redhawk was in there, but Greyson rarely ever called that number.

The man answered on the second ring.

"Wondered when I'd hear from you," Redhawk said immediately.

"Rachel and I been up to no good," Greyson replied, letting the man know where everyone sat on this one. "Need you to do me a favor. It's a really mean one, so I figure you'll like it."

"Oh?"

"Has anyone called Zielinski and let him know that his old buddy Fred Jansen got hit by a truck last night?" Greyson asked in as innocent a tone as he could manage without rolling his eyes. "That he's in the hospital right now?"

Rachel did roll hers as she watched and listened.

Redhawk was silent for a long moment.

"You know what?" he finally said. "I don't think so. Should we correct that oversight?"

"I managed to locate an interesting piece of evidence last night when we went by Jansen's place for clean clothes," Greyson said. "Haven't entered it into the evidence tracking system yet, but I'm kind of in hot pursuit right now."

"According to the train schedule, you should be arriving in Jacksonville any minute," Redhawk pointed out, letting Greyson know that the man was on top of things up north. "If we call, Zielinski might just have time to make it to the airport as you crossed the panhandle. You would probably miss him."

"That would be a shame," Greyson cried crocodile tears. "I doubt that the man would be armed if you needed to take him into custody at the hospital or if he swung by the Bureau office in Boston, but you might keep it in the back of your mind for later."

"What did you find?" Redhawk asked sharply.

"A thread," Greyson said. It was pretty much an honest and straightforward answer. "I'm tugging on it right now to see what might unravel when I do."

"I see," Redhawk replied. "And you didn't call Parsons because?"

"She's not as paranoid as you are." Greyson smiled. "At least not yet. Still getting her feet underneath her and this will rattle the entire office a whole bunch. Best if she can blame those damned politicians in DC for meddling, right?"

"I do like the way you think, Leigh," Redhawk laughed. "And I'll keep both ladies in the loop. Anything else you needed?"

"Nope," Greyson said. "Next call will probably be in about three hours, so I'm likely to interrupt a late dinner, knowing Denise's regular schedule. But I'll know more then."

"Will you have the case solved by then?" Redhawk asked, his voice turning deadly serious now.

"Not making any promises," Greyson replied.

He hung up without any other comments and looked closely at Rachel.

"Now's when it gets ugly?" she asked.

"Now," Greyson agreed. "Everything up until this has been merely the antipasti."

"That's what frightens me," she nodded.

[23]

BOLTHOLE

GREYSON KNEW THAT PANAMA CITY WAS A DIFFERENT world from the rest of Florida. Hell, it was far more like the nearby parts of Georgia and Alabama, just north across the old state lines that didn't mean all that much anymore, than it was like Orlando or Miami.

Old Confederacy, even today, two centuries after the *Lost Cause* that had never quite flamed out enough to finally just do everyone a favor and die. The farther east and south you got from here, the more cosmopolitan and touristy things got, but this chunk of the state had never gotten that memo.

Greyson didn't want to call it backwards, but it was. Insular might be a better term. Running on an older clock that hadn't really adapted well to the arrival of aliens. Hell, parts of the area hasn't really adapted well to losing the Civil War.

It had been a retirement kind of community for a long time, but retirement for folks just making enough from a pension or savings to hang on, rather than living large. You moved to Jacksonville or Miami/Dade for that sort of thing.

These were the office workers from up north that had hit

the magic age number and then moved to the Gulf Coast to slowly die in the sun.

From Tallahassee, he and Rachel had caught a local train down here and checked into a hotel. Greyson had offered to get two rooms, but Rachel had been fine with a single as long as it had two queen beds. Otherwise he might have insisted.

Greyson didn't need that complication, and wasn't going to even ask at this point.

They had rented a car as well, so they could get around, and just finished eating dinner at a local dive that catered to tourists, so seafood that wasn't that great, but let you tell folks back home that it was authentic.

Probably just about as authentic as the boxes it might have been served from in Kansas City, but he wasn't going to complain. It was good enough and he didn't have delicate or educated tastes, in spite of what Emmy had attempted with him.

"Now what?" Rachel asked as they got into the car and looked around the parking lot of *The Hungry Shak*.

Greyson studied the sun through the few clouds that were breaking up. Panama City faced more or less south, so the sky was just starting to turn red as it set over the water in the southwest.

He keyed his comm.

Redhawk answered immediately. Again.

"Zielinski just boarded a red-eye flight from Tallahassee to Boston about ten minutes ago," Edgar said instead of anything prosaic, like *hello*. "They'll be in the air in about thirty minutes and here around midnight."

"He make any calls locally after whoever talked to him?" Greyson asked, mostly on a lark.

But you never knew. Redhawk might have managed to put some serious resources on tracking the man once he knew what Greyson and Rachel were up to.

"None that matter," Redhawk said in an offhand manner that suggested they had been recorded at the time and reviewed for evidence immediately afterwards.

A little frightening, but that was the flip side of the modern world. Everything bound up in a single, electronic whole made it fast and efficient to talk and buy things, but it also made it simple to track someone's life once you targeted them with law enforcement tools.

Calling Quinton Laux for some help keeping private things private sounded more and more useful. Greyson wondered when he'd gotten so paranoid, but he knew the answer to that.

The day he had developed secrets worth being killed over.

"We'll move forward from here," Greyson said.

"You're still in the Eastern Metroplex," Redhawk reminded him obliquely.

"And Zielinski is probably good pals and drinking buddies with the chief of police down here, knowing him," Greyson countered. "I'll take my chances talking to any beat cops that get called. Parsons can always come rescue me tomorrow if she has to get me out of jail. Denise needs to be protected."

"Oh, she is," Redhawk said sternly. "Trust me on that."

"Will do," Greyson said and hung up.

Edgar Redhawk wasn't kidding, either. He'd fall on his own sword if it became necessary rather than allow any of this to splash his boss. He'd been the same way with Owens, until it became clear just how bent the man was and that nothing was going to save him from Denise.

Nothing that had ever come out publicly, but the Metropolitan had given several of her Police Commissioners the options of retirement quietly or prosecution noisily when the shit started rolling downhill. Everyone had wisely seen it her way and packed their desks.

Edgar Redhawk was a political creature, but a loyal one. When his old boss had been taken down, Denise had hired him and he'd given her the exact same loyalty.

Probably better, since she was honest and Redhawk wouldn't have to hold his nose at too many things.

Tonight might be stretching it, but they were in pursuit of justice.

Just not doing it according to the book.

Or rather, the *Book of Greyson Leigh* instead.

He looked at Rachel.

"You're navigating," he said as he flipped the car on and checked the batteries. Full charge and everything responding as it should.

"North on Beck here," she pointed at the road in front of them. "It'll take us past Pretty Bayou and up to Lynn Haven. We'll catch State Road 77 across the bridge and over the top of Fanning Bayou. He lives in what looks like a dump on the edge of a town called Southport, on the other side of the bayou itself."

While Greyson got them in motion, she programmed the nav system and they were off, listening to the car beep at him with things he was supposed to do.

It was weird, driving on roads laid out on a proper, Jeffersonian grid, but he'd spent too much time in Boston where all the roads were crooked, and before that in places once categorized as the Third World. Back before all of Earth turned out to be a backwater, much like Panama City was today.

He drove them further into the past as they headed north. The rain earlier in the day over on the Atlantic coast had given way, but things were still gray and a little overcast on the Gulf coast once the sun got low enough.

Greyson hadn't thought about storms, but the hurricanes were more frequent and more intense than they'd been when he was a kid. A lot of the retirees were having to move farther inland every year, or build houses like fortresses if they wanted to stay on the beach.

As they got closer to their destination, Greyson could see the evidence of change. A good Gulf hurricane would push a lot of water up this bayou, and he wasn't sure how high a surge might go.

The place where Zielinski lived looked like it had been left to the elements. Greyson could see marks that might be super high tides leaving moss and salt stains on the cinder block bricks that made up the bottom of the various buildings and covering most of the parking lot about axle deep on most cars.

Four stories of flats facing out over the parking lot, with external walkways across the front. Maybe fifty units, all told, as it stretched around a corner like an *L*. Air conditioners were local to each unit, but at least the Illymus Merchant Guild had been able to provide humanity a new set of alien technologies that made such things small and hyper-efficient, without making the planet any warmer.

It would still be the rest of his lifetime and maybe all of Rachel's before the planet started cooling down again, but hopefully they'd managed to save it in time.

Not that the people he could see from here would benefit. Or even much care.

He parked and got out. Rachel was a beat ahead of him.

"We know he's gone," she said. "Do we pick the lock or ask the manager?"

"I don't think a guy like Zielinski is going to go out of his way to be friendly with folks, so I doubt that anyone here cares," Greyson said. "But they might call the cops anyway, and those people are probably the only locals he gets along with."

He set off for the manager's office, noting that the lights were still on.

He knocked and a sour-faced Anglo woman opened the inner door, scowling up at him through the glass storm door.

Greyson flashed his badge at her and smiled grimly.

She opened the storm door just enough that they didn't have to yell at each other.

"Yeah?" she asked.

"I'd like to look in the apartment of one of your tenants who isn't home," he said simply.

"Got a warrant?" she asked sourly, just like she was supposed to.

"We're Hunters," Greyson said, waggling the badge case just a little to draw her eye to it. "We chase dangerous aliens and kill them. Do I need to go get a warrant and maybe waste your entire week and tear your property apart looking for my answers, or do you want to do things quietly? Your choice."

He was only sort of bluffing. She could legitimately push back right now. He'd call Redhawk and have a warrant in his hands in minutes.

But that would start a clock ticking, because the chances were extremely good that someone somewhere would notice and place a call to Zielinski when his name popped up on a screen. He was in the air right now, but they'd reach him eventually.

At that point, either the man would start calling in favors or blackmail. Things would get very ugly, or very public.

Maybe both.

"Who?" the woman asked after a moment.

"Olek Zielinski," Greyson smiled at her.

This was the magic moment in the adventure.

How did she feel about the man?

"That son of a bitch?" she rasped angrily. "What's that shitbird done now?"

Bingo.

You could never really go wrong, expecting Zielinski to be an asshole to people.

He just didn't have that badge anymore protecting him from the consequences.

"We'd like to look in his place as part of an ongoing investigation," Rachel spoke up, sounding helpful and polite.

Greyson didn't have it in him right now.

"Stay put," she said, leaving the inner door open as she stepped over and grabbed a key ring out of a bowl nearby.

The woman was wearing house slippers and an old, faded sundress as she stepped out into the gathering gloom. Night birds and bug zappers competed in a symphony to fill the night with noise. The air was a little sticky with heat and humidity, but nothing he minded.

"Follow me," she commanded in a tired voice.

Greyson put her age at somewhere close enough to dead, except that she looked like the kind of woman who would go down with Satan's throat in her teeth when he finally came for her.

She led them up to the third level and halfway across to an apartment with a dark window. The place reminded Greyson of an old roadside motel, now that he thought about it. Maybe it had gone out of business and been converted into cheap apartments at some point?

None of the units were very wide, nor deep. The side building that made the base of the *L* looked like a later addition, with doors farther apart, so maybe those were all two bedroom and this wing was studio? That felt right.

She looked in the window and nodded, muttering a never-ending string of profanities that didn't once appear to repeat as Greyson listened, which was pretty impressive. Maybe she'd been a Marine in her sordid youth?

"He's not home," she announced.

"Yes," Greyson said. "We've more or less tricked him into flying to Boston for an emergency, so we had time to see what we might find here."

"You going to take his punk ass down hard?" She seemed to light up and turn into a younger woman when she asked, so Greyson assumed a history there that he didn't pursue.

"That's our hope," Rachel said professionally, playing an admirable job of good cop.

Greyson wasn't sure what the next step *beyond* Bad Cop looked like, but he was probably there. At least in his mind.

"Here," the manager said, unlocking the door and stepping back as she opened it. "You folks let me know if you need anything else to ruin that fucker's day."

She turned and departed without looking back, like maybe she didn't want to be an accessory.

Greyson listened, but didn't hear a dog rustling around in the darkness. Didn't smell a cat's funk.

He reached inside and flipped on the overhead light.

Sterile.

Even worse than Jansen's place had been. Greyson wondered if the apartment had come with furniture already and Zielinski had just put his clothes in the dresser. If the place had once been a motel, that logic might fit.

Just inside the door was a bedroom. Or a bed on the left with a floral bedcover and nightstands on each side. Dresser on the right, just past where the door opened.

He slipped in and moved to close the curtains against unwelcome peepers. Rachel closed the door and looked around.

"Yuck," she pronounced unequivocally.

Greyson nodded and moved deeper. There was a

bathroom midway back. Standard box with a toilet and a tub that had a shower head and a nylon curtain.

The back of the apartment had the first impression of personality that Greyson had seen. He'd been expecting a sofa, but there was a desk instead, and a comfortable chair just beyond it, lined up to face a screen next to the half-sized kitchen that was just big enough to be called one.

He looked in the fridge, and was not the least bit surprised. Leftover takeout and bottles of cheap beer. The freezer held frozen dinners and a lot of ice.

"Greyson."

Something in Rachel's voice had his hand on his nerve scrambler before he was fully around again.

She was kneeling in the corner. There was a table there, but she was looking under it.

"Here," she pointed.

Greyson moved close and knelt.

File cabinet. Custom made from the look of it, with three normal-sized drawers across, and three half-height ones above them so it could fit the lowered space under the table.

You couldn't see anything from the patio's sliding glass door, and the desk and chair obscured it from the front.

Greyson felt his heart sink as he considered what might be in the thing.

He rose and closed the curtain nearby as well, turning on a light with the outdoor glow gone. The floor in here was tile. The walls were covered over with that bamboo paneling that looked like wood.

It felt more like an office than a living room.

Olek just slept up front. He lived back here. Worked here.

Plotted his revenge here.

"Check it for power and wires coming out," he ordered her. "Alarms or something."

"What about the lock?" she asked, starting to rifle around the back and sides while he watched.

Greyson looked close. Old-fashioned mechanical lock you opened with a key. Probably on a ring in Zielinski's pocket right now, about fifteen thousand meters up and northbound.

There had to be a spare. Or he could just steal the damned thing, but Greyson would have expected Zielinski to bolt it to the floor or something. He would have.

Greyson rose and studied the room. He moved to the desk, but it wasn't locked. No reason to, if you had a better setup over there. Each drawer was opened and inspected anyway, but he was dealing with an ex-cop who would think like one. And be expecting someone to try to break in at some point.

Where would I hide a key?

A brass ashtray on top of the desk caught his eye for reasons that his conscious mind didn't grasp. Not that big. Not that hefty. He'd have made something like this with three or four times as much metal. This was a thin disk tilted up all the way around the rim, with four spots on the cardinal points where you could rest a cigar.

The basin was filled with cheap ash, in keeping with Zielinski and his lifestyle. Greyson didn't think the man was poor, as corrupt as he had been.

Even after paying bribes and kickbacks he had been raking it in, if Greyson's investigations that had gotten shut down had been anything remotely accurate.

No, he just smoked cheap Cubans. Olek Zielinski did everything cheap.

A number etched on the side of the ashtray finally got his attention.

207.

Son of a bitch.

"What?" Rachel stood up from where she had been kneeling, also going for a pistol. Palmstunner in her case, but still…

Greyson touched the ash tray with one angry finger to indicate it.

"Two Oh Seven," he said.

"Why is that important?" Rachel asked as she stepped up next to him.

"That was my badge number, once upon a time," Greyson said. "What do you want to bet that this was my actual badge? Maybe melted down with a blowtorch and bashed into shape? The records said it had been *lost* at some point. I have Two Nineteen now."

He looked at it, thin brass and all. Yeah, about as much metal as he had in his current badge.

Greyson lifted the ashtray up and considered Olek Zielinski. There was a trashcan under the desk, and all the ashes were currently cool, so he turned it a little sideways and started to shake the ashes out into the can.

It wasn't like Zielinski would be ignorant that someone was in here. Especially not if Greyson ended up making a call and having him arrested at Jansen's bedside.

A scraping sound got his attention. Rather than make more of a mess, he grabbed a pen and flicked the rest of ash into the trash can.

There was a key, buried in those ashes. Right where nobody would think to look if they didn't have a connection to 207.

And who would except a Hunter named Greyson Leigh? Or a retired asshole named Olek Zielinski?

Retired Hunter, rather. He was still an asshole. Greyson had no doubt about that.

Greyson took the key and walked over to the sink. He washed it clean and handed it to Rachel with a grimace.

"That's probably the spare," he said simply.

"You two have a scary love/hate relationship," Rachel observed.

"Ain't no love there, Rachel," he replied.

"Yeah, I see that," she said, taking the key and kneeling by the cabinet.

The lock turned smoothly and she pulled the first drawer open as he got down on his knees next to her.

She opened the middle drawer while he randomly pulled out a file and began looking at it.

"Son of a bitch," he muttered, wondering how often he was going to repeat himself tonight.

"What?"

"Recognize the handwriting?" he asked, laying the file flat for her.

"Looks like yours?" Rachel asked carefully, studying the long hieroglyphics that he routinely put on paper with a pen.

Just one of the reasons he preferred typing on a keyboard.

"It is mine," he said. "This was part of an investigation I was running two years ago, before I got shut down. Zielinski made them disappear from Records."

"All this your stuff?" she gestured to the others.

"Dunno," Greyson said, sliding the file back and reaching into the middle.

The particular file he happened to grab said Kwan. He opened it up and confirmed that it was Head Police Commissioner Yulia Kwan. She was an older woman than Greyson by a few years. A Vladivostok Russian/Hong Kong Mix that had always reminded him of the actress Michelle Yeoh, except nearly a foot taller. Almost as beautiful, though.

More pictures. Yulia in the middle of an orgy, from the way the bodies were arranged on a big bed. Yulia being seriously dominated by a woman who looked like a stone pro, from the expensive gear that Yulia was tied to and being beaten with.

Greyson didn't have those sorts of kinks, but he understood that a lot of extremely powerful politicians flipped end-for-end in their private lives. Looked from these photos that Yulia Kwan got her rocks off as a sub.

Nothing wrong with it on the surface, but these were the sorts of pictures you blackmailed someone with. Ruined their career by leaking them to the press or the opposition.

Greyson wondered if any of those three strapping men, filling all of her holes at once, were criminals of some sort. They all had ink that suggested Russian mafia, and Vladivostok was known as an underworld hub.

There was a story here, if he wished to pursue it.

Greyson put it back and looked for other files. Buford Owens apparently had a monumental addiction to a variety of narcotics, some of which were even legal, but most of which were good for time in the county pen. Especially in the sorts of dosages the man must be running on a daily basis.

He almost qualified as a dealer, except that he was consuming it all himself.

Greyson rocked back on his heels and wondered if the rest of this was all the blackmail material Zielinski had managed to accumulate in a lifetime as a corrupt cop, first in Chicago and later in Boston as a Hunter.

"There are a lot of lives fucked if this comes out, aren't there?" Rachel asked.

Greyson flinched. He'd almost forgotten the young woman was sitting next to him.

He nodded mutely. There was a file for Denise Upkins at the back, properly alphabetized, but Greyson couldn't bring himself to look in it. How many pictures of him would

Greyson find? Olek knew what he'd done for a living for the twenty years before he joined the force.

Greyson had understood that reporters poking at any sort of public relationship between the two of them would have raised uncomfortable questions, so they had ended it.

Was Zielinski all set to ruin her life?

Olek had managed to frame Greyson. Not hard to get people to see things your way if you had their balls in a vice with these files.

He'd been set up as a fall guy, because Owens and Kwan had both understood that it was their careers or Leigh's.

Greyson considered how he might destroy all of them, just as payback for the time off he'd been forced to take. Denise had managed to backdate him for seniority when he returned, so his pension was back on track, if he wanted to stay another eight years to collect a double-twenty.

Live high on the hog in places like Miami/Dade, perhaps?

"Greyson?" Rachel asked hesitantly.

He turned to her and shook his whole body against the sudden chill that had descended.

He'd always suspected that Olek Zielinski was even worse than anyone ever gave him credit for, but now he had proof.

"We're taking it all," Greyson announced, pulling out the nearest drawer and unlocking the slide so he could stand up with it.

"We burning it or turning it in?" she pressed.

"I'll know that tomorrow," he said. "After we read it all."

[24]

SECRETS

Rachel kept watch in the apartment while Greyson hauled those heavy file drawers down to the car and locked them in the trunk. Not that they didn't trust the neighborhood, but at some point this was likely to turn into a chain of evidence question and she wanted to be able to say that they had things as covered as best they could, given the circumstances.

Greyson had freaked the fuck out at the contents of some of those files. She had too, to a lesser degree, but she didn't have any sort of personal relationship with most of the names, so they were just victims with strange kinks, as far as she was concerned.

It was the top drawers that had caused the most problems.

Rachel had opened one of them and found a ghost gun. Looked new. Didn't have a serial number. Ghost was an old term for a firearm manufactured without any serial number at all, like they had done back in the Nineteenth Century.

For a long time, the law had required such things stamped on, just so guns used in crimes could be traced back to points of sale. That had changed about the time Greyson was a kid if she had the ancient history right.

Three-dimensional printing had started off with spools of plastic that you could feed in hot and a computer would slowly assemble something in layers. Mostly kitsch, but all early tech seemed to follow a path through hobbyists doing things before working their way up to serious usefulness.

Over the decades, the technology and the materials had gotten better, so that you could print a working gun.

The fabs required were still huge, but it was possible to dial up a design and tell a box about the size of the car they'd driven here to pull raw materials from stores and do things with it.

And if the place was an illegal shop, or maybe one working after hours, they didn't necessarily stamp or print a serial number on the frame.

Zielinski had what Rachel would have called a pocket pistol in there. Slugthrower, which were generally illegal in private possession, since you were supposed to store them at the gun range you belonged to.

But a cop has ways of working the system, especially when he knows the people charged with enforcing them.

Semi-automatic. 9mm with fifteen rounds stagger-stacked in the grip. The bullets themselves had started life as ball ammunition. Rounded copper tips designed to penetrate like an ice pick. But these had been chopped a little, taking just enough off the tip to expose the lead underneath in an area about four millimeters across.

Rachel supposed they might qualify as a form of jacketed softnose, but that just meant that shooting someone would cause it to expand like a flower as it went through their body.

The plates and kevlar she had under her shirt would save her from anything but a nasty bruise, assuming someone didn't shoot her in the face or the ass.

Didn't prove that Zielinski had been the one behind the hit, but it did sink his sorry ass in a ripe pool of shit. That guy in Boston had been shooting with a ghost revolver, rather than a sliding semi-auto, but just possession of an illegal gun in the hands of a civilian like Zielinski was a good enough charge, regardless of what else they found in the files.

The only thing they hadn't found on a quick skim of the place had been evidence of the Synth Chip that the perp had been using.

Did that mean that Zielinski had hired it out? Blackmailed someone for it? Or was there a safety deposit box somewhere else with more evidence?

The latter didn't feel right to Rachel. Captain Zielinski had been the kind of guy who would want it all where he could see it and touch it at all times.

Control freak.

The front door was closed but not locked. Enough to keep civilians out of this crime scene while she watched the files and Greyson hauled things.

Rachel stood in the exact center of the room and looked around.

Where would I hide something?

It would be in here. The front and the bathroom had been anonymous places. Zielinski didn't live there. He just slept and bathed.

Whatever it was would be in this room.

Desk. Chair. Table. File cabinet. Stove that didn't look used. Microwave overhead. Refrigerator. Couple of bookshelves with curios, but nothing personal. Crap you picked up as a memento of a trip because you'd stuffed it in the suitcase when you were packing to go home, and never gotten around to throwing it in the trash.

She looked inside a couple of the books, mindful that the file cabinet key had been hidden under the cigar ashes.

Nothing in the books. No notes tucked in or centers of pages chopped out.

Too much like a spy thriller anyway. Zielinski was a spider at the center of a web. Hide it in plain sight because he's smarter than everyone else and putting one over on them.

Except that he's dealing with Greyson Leigh and Rachel Asher now. We're smarter than he is, right?

She moved to the refrigerator, thinking back to her first case as Greyson's partner. The blond with the big tits that the Phrenic had used as a vector to get into Dominguez's apartment.

Her refrigerator had been similarly empty, because she had takeout delivered regularly, instead of cooking.

Cooking.

Rachel turned to the stove and opened the oven door to peek inside. Old and gnarly, but with dust, not grime.

How the hell does a stove get dusty?

Unless it was never used.

Something clicked in the back of her head and she turned back to the freezer section of the refrigerator. Opened the door and peered at the boxes of dinners stashed in there. Four of them. The top one looked fine. Salisbury steak, potatoes, and an apple pie thing in an aluminum tray.

Not something you can nuke, with all that metal, so you have to cook it in the oven.

But you never cook.

Rachel slid it to one side and noted that the other three had some serious ice build up going. She checked expiration dates and noted that the middle one was supposedly bad three years ago.

Three years?

Zielinski had only been here for a little under seven months now. Who wouldn't have emptied the junk out of the freezer before he moved in?

She pulled it out of the pile and realized how much heavier it was than the others.

Rachel felt her mouth go dry as she walked back to the table, closing the freezer door behind her. She put the TV dinner box down and saw where the edge that had been on the back side when it was in the freezer was taped shut with the invisible stuff you used on presents.

She reached into a pocket and came out with a knife that she flipped open, slicing the taped edge and hoping her pounding heart wouldn't cause her to flinch and cut herself.

Last thing she needed was to bleed all over the crime scene and have the punks from Forensics give her crap. Even podunks like this county would have on staff.

But then, were they really going to call in the local authorities? Greyson had been talking to Edgar Redhawk before they broke in here. And had stopped.

They were removing all this evidence and putting it in the car. Was Greyson about to suddenly drive back to Boston in the rental?

How fucking weird was this case about to get?

Weirder? Was that grammatically allowed?

Something. She'd ask an English major next time she saw one, if she remembered.

The back of the box was open. She put the knife down instead of trying to close the folding blade. That was just asking to bleed.

Instead, she reached for the flap and pulled it open. The box was heavy, so she tipped it and dumped a pile of heavy pages into her hand.

Rachel gasped when she saw what they were.

[25]

CHAIN OF EVIDENCE

GREYSON HEARD RACHEL GASPING AS HE OPENED THE door. She was looking at something on the table over the file cabinets.

He closed the door behind him and locked it. For good measure, he chirped the car locks again, because it felt like something big had just happened.

"You okay?" he called as he walked to the back of the apartment.

"No," Rachel replied in a flat, hard voice.

No pain in her voice, so he wasn't reaching for his comm to call for an ambulance or a pistol to shoot someone.

She sounded mad as hell. Rachel didn't get there very often. When she did, smart people ran for the hills.

Greyson walked close enough to look over her shoulder.

Yeah, that would probably do it.

"How many?" he asked, reaching out a hand and picking up the top bearer instrument off a stack of them.

You ran into them from time to time. Mostly when people wanted a legal way to move money around in an era when banks had to report anything with that many zeroes to an artificial intelligence system that would look for suggestions of a crime.

Anonymous. Allowed the bearer to present it at any point and convert the document in hand to a number of shares of stock in a corporation or a stack of bonds. Presumably, ones that had been dumping interest or dividends into a bank account somewhere that still didn't like playing well with banking regulators.

It had been island nations in the Caribbean when Greyson was young. Now there were several countries that dealt directly with the aliens and happily told the blustering politicians in North America or Europe to piss off.

Greyson recognized the company named on the top document as he slipped it to one side. Major software manufacturer. The one under it made cars. Several pages dealing with government and municipal bonds. Transportation companies.

Greyson whistled when he assembled the whole into an image in his head. Maybe thirty or forty million loonies worth of value here, depending on the market. Mark that down a little for the bribes you'd have to pay to cash them in without raising a fuss.

Still a shit ton of money. Especially for a retired cop from Chicago.

From the chicken fried steak dinner box on the table, they'd been stored in the freezer. Another trick like putting the key in the ash tray.

Rachel turned a pale face up at him now.

"Honest cops?" she asked in a timid, withdrawn voice.

He studied her eyes, dilated about as far as they could go in this light.

"Mostly," he replied. "If the population can't trust us to do the job, they have other troubles. Why?"

"This is fuck-you-money, Greyson," she said. "Evidence

of crimes on a scale I don't think I can imagine, even after the classes I've been taking. What have we stepped into and how do we get it off our boots?"

"I'm not sure yet," he offered her.

It was at least an honest assessment of things. He'd come down here looking for clues that would lead him to a fabrication plant. The black kind that had made an illegal Synth Chip that turned everyday people into assassins. The threads connecting the shooter to Olek had been tenuous, but held up each time he tugged at them in his mind.

"Not sure yet?" she asked, covering her mouth in shock at how loud she'd suddenly gotten.

He gestured to the stack in the box.

"We already knew he was bent, Rachel," Greyson said. "Hell, my investigations that happened to start pointing in his direction on a completely unrelated case is what got me ousted the first time. Nobody could ever make anything stick, because he could lean on the people who might have otherwise decided to prosecute the man."

Zielinski could destroy lives with the sorts of things Greyson had seen in the files he'd stashed in the sedan's trunk.

But what could Zielinski do if he didn't have those files?

And was the world a better place with them public or destroyed?

That was the genesis of Rachel's question.

Burn it or unleash it?

The moral and legal answer involved calling Redhawk right now and having him scramble a team of bloodthirsty beavers to wade through the forest of evidence.

On the other hand, the bearer instruments were just that: entitlements to the bearer of the document to cash or equivalent value on presentation. None of them had names, either. Just issuance numbers for tracking purposes, so you couldn't easily forge them or make duplicate copies.

He or Rachel could retire to a life of debaucherous luxury with what was in his hand. Like Dominguez and that closet full of bespoke suits when he'd been killed.

"I'm finally nervous," Rachel admitted as Greyson did all the calculus in his head.

"Me, too," he admitted as well. "This isn't an assassination anymore. This is something huge, and we just happened to avoid being collateral damage at the outset."

"Zielinski clearing the decks?" she asked. "Get rid of us before he goes after Upkins and whoever else was in his way or owed him for the pain you put him through?"

"Don't know," Greyson replied. "Won't without a confession. Not sure I could actually get him to admit it on tape."

"How would you even try?" Rachel asked, surprised.

Greyson smiled as a plan took shape in his head.

"They say *in vino veritas*," Greyson told her. "*In wine you find truth*. A drunk man will no longer shade what he thinks or how he feels."

"You're going to get Captain Zielinski drunk?" she gasped.

Greyson smiled at his partner.

"It works just as well when you make someone very, *very* angry."

[26]

TIMEBOMB

GREYSON WONDERED IF THOSE FILES WERE A FORM OF infectious disease. Once you had them, you were unwilling to ever let them out of your sight again, like that character in the fable with the pile of gold coins.

Greyson and Rachel had loaded all the evidence into the trunk of the rental, then swept the place one more time for any last surprises and to make sure that they hadn't left any fingerprints behind. The chicken fried steak had felt like the last bomb in Zielinski's arsenal. Everything else could be stored in a bank's safety deposit box against need. False identify cards, spare bundles of cash, whatever. The sorts of things you put in a bug-out bag for the end of the world.

Whether it was the whole world or just yours when the cops suddenly started closing in and you had to run for the hills. Or someplace that didn't like Americans that much and might not honor an extradition request.

Greyson couldn't let the car out of his sight. He knew that. Rachel didn't understand, but she didn't have the history of crap with Zielinski that Greyson had been forced to wade through over the years, either.

They'd gone as far as the hotel and checked right back out, suffering the cost of one night's unused stay but Greyson didn't care. That wasn't going to break the bank and he could probably get it reimbursed anyway.

He'd looked at a map as they sat parked in front of one of those all-night diners. The greasy kind with a full wall of windows all the way across the front to let in light during the day and illuminate the parking lot at night. Greyson parked where he could watch the car from inside and then headed in, Rachel in tow.

The place had been a chain, once upon a time. Before the Illymus Merchant Guild came along from the night sky and messed up the entire planet by trying to make it a better place. Faster planes, faster trains, and electric robot cars meant that fewer folks had to stop regularly to stretch their legs on long trips, or add petroleum to an internal combustion engine to make it go.

A lot of roadside diners hadn't survived. Or, like this one, had reinvented themselves as truly local dives. He'd checked the parking lot for license plates when he pulled in. Almost all local, or he'd have kept driving.

Fools from out of state might not know any better than to eat here, but if you had locals, the food had to be pretty good.

In honor of Olek Jan Zielinski, Greyson ordered the chicken fried steak breakfast, even this late in the evening, going on midnight. Eggs over easy. The really runny kind you mopped up with some sourdough toast. Hash browns extra crispy, until they were more like soggy potato chips than anything. And gravy made with an even mixture of pork sausage and bacon. Weird, but he'd already made a note to find a joint in Boston that did it that way, just based on the waitress's description.

If it was any good, he'd have to find a recipe and ask one of the places back home to add it to menu.

Rachel had to watch out for her girlish, weight-lifter's figure, so she'd gone with protein on a salad. Chicken Waldorf. The woman was probably as strong as he was, but she worked out with iron while Greyson focused on walking long distances and running up and down stairs instead.

They had both ordered a slice of fresh coffee and were sitting there contemplating the night.

What sorts of pheromones the two of them were giving off wasn't something Greyson could understand, but just like on the train, the woman up front had taken one look at them and seated them off in a corner away from everyone else.

Like maybe they were on a date or something? Did people bring dates to this roadside dive?

Greyson had learned early on that you never took a date to dinner the first time you went out. Too easy to look like a dork or spill something on yourself embarrassingly. Take her to a movie. Or the park. Emmy had been seduced by a museum, but Greyson suspected that it wouldn't have taken much, since she had come chasing after him.

Dinner was for after they knew you were secretly a nerd. Emmy had kept him around.

"So now what are we doing?" Rachel asked in a casual, off-hand kind of voice belied by the seriousness in her eyes. "Obviously, we're not staying in Panama City. What kind of danger are we in?"

"Us?" Greyson blinked, returning to the present from all the deep and twisted things he had been contemplating. "None. This is all about the trouble we're going to drop on other people."

"That bad?" Her eyes lit up now with a little more fire. Like maybe she got off on that aspect of law enforcement. He hadn't pried too deeply into the woman.

"It might be," he temporized instead. "We haven't looked through those files to really see all Zielinski's victims, so I have no idea how many lives he might have been able to destroy if he wanted to. A bunch and badly is just a rough guess. Publicly, too. Plus, if we do dig, the kind of thing where you get warrants and take Olek's entire life apart meticulously, I'm pretty sure we'd be able to trace all those bearer instruments back to the people who had been paying him, under the table either as blackmail or protection money against it. Again, more lives destroyed."

"Aren't we supposed to be the good guys, Greyson?" Rachel grimaced.

"We are," he agreed. "What's good in this? Outing all those people for having their kinks as part of taking Zielinski down? Utterly shattering the entire bureaucratic structure of the Eastern Metroplex government by showing how deep the rot has gotten? Or letting those people know we have the files and forcing more and more of them to resign so that maybe folks can be promoted that aren't compromised."

"There are no good answers, are there?"

He watched her take another bite of coffee.

"I personally don't care that Yulia Kwan seems to like it three or four on one," Greyson said. "Or that she probably gets off on other people watching her when she does. We all have our kinks. The blackmail makes it impossible for her to continue in any office, anywhere. Owens was the same way."

"He got anything on Upkins?" Rachel asked.

It sounded innocent, but to Greyson it was still a knife to the guts.

Did Zielinski have anything that might have compromised Denise? Wouldn't he have used it to keep his old job? Or had Zielinski used it instead to ensure that she didn't come after him when he had retired?

Greyson knew exactly how many years it had been since the two of the had been intimate, but he hadn't really known the political side of her all that much then. Just the incredible mind housed in that amazing body, and where she liked to be kissed. And other things.

But he hadn't been able to bring himself to look in that file yet. Just couldn't do it.

Owens, like Kwan, had been compromised. Pills of so many different kinds and effects that Greyson wondered how the man hadn't just accidentally undergone spontaneous human combustion at any point.

It must take a doctor using an AI just to keep him looking like he was intact.

And Redhawk had moved right up from being Owens's right hand to being Denise's. What did that say about the situation, except that power almost always corrupted?

Even Greyson felt the tug, like little fishies nibbling at his toes. He should have called Redhawk already and turned everything in. Photos. Lists. Databases. Bearer Instruments.

Put the whole thing into evidence and let the chips fall where they might.

Who was he protecting? Denise, but did she really need it?

Hard to say. Really, what he had was a rendezvous with destiny in the form of Zielinski.

"Greyson?" Rachel spoke again, like maybe he'd missed her the first time. Or somehow forgotten about the woman sitting across from him.

"I don't know, Rachel," he finally replied, wondering how many heartbeats had passed.

"So how are we going to play this?" she pursued.

"I'd like to fill up on food," Greyson said. "It's about twenty-three hundred kilometers to Boston from here and I'd like to turn off our comms, turn on the robot, and let it drive us autonomously. Sleep in the car. Hit the occasional drive-through and rest stops between here and there, and we can slip in early afternoon tomorrow. Stop long enough to shower and change clothes, and then ask Redhawk to arrest Zielinski wherever he is, but only when we can land on him like a ton of bricks before he can do anything to wriggle free."

"How do we stop him from lawyering up and stone-walling everything?" Rachel asked, shifting now from Hunter to Boss mode.

"The Official Secrets Act," Greyson smiled viciously.

"How's that going to help?" She sat back with a look of confusion on her face and drank some more coffee.

He joined her drinking as he ordered his thoughts.

"Accusing him of being a spy means he gets dropped into a small box with very few rights, Rachel," Greyson explained. "Doesn't matter who he might be spying on or for. Spies are assumed to be flight risks and dangers to the community, so they get hard isolation immediately. It will take a while before anybody can prove anything to let him come back as far as normal criminal rights. I figure we can break him long before then, especially if it has my name on it."

"How much of his files are you likely to show Redhawk?" she smiled grimly now, understanding where he was headed. "He'll have to know what's going on."

"That's what the long drive is for," Greyson nodded. "We pull the files up into the back seat just before we leave and then spend our time reading and cataloging them, so we have a list of names when we get to Boston."

"We destroying everyone and everything?" Rachel's eyes got dark.

"Not if I can help it," he replied.

"Then what?" she asked.

"I want to take Zielinski down," Greyson said. "Hard and permanent. Then we'll burn everything. I don't expect that there is anyone we can trust with that evidence."

"Nobody?"

"Nobody."

[27]

REST STOP

PARTLY TO AVOID MAJOR CITIES, AND PARTLY FOR THE view itself, Greyson had programmed the car to take them up to Birmingham, Alabama, then loop northeast through Chattanooga and Knoxville. Places he'd never even done more than fly over. Through Roanoke, they were able to pass through Harrisburg and Allentown before dropping into New Jersey and circling New York City clockwise without ever entering.

Then again north, instead of direct. They were outside Springfield, Mass right now, stretching their legs by walking all the way around a rest area and getting a cup of the volunteer-supplied coffee. It wasn't even that nasty tasting, but Greyson had only catnapped in between reading files and hitting a chain burger joint for breakfast burritos a few hours ago.

They hit the farthest back corner of the triangular shaped trees and grass and turned back. Nobody was within a hundred meters except a dog going madly after a ball someone had launched with a jai lai stick.

"You suppose they know where we are?" Rachel asked innocently.

She looked like hell from the lack of good sleep causing bags under her eyes. Not as bad as he felt, but she had youth to carry her. He just had bile.

"Probably," he said. "Redhawk will have tried to call when we didn't call him back last night. It went straight to voice mail. After a couple of those, he probably turned on the highway scanner and typed our license plate into the system."

"So he knows we're headed home, and what road we're on," Rachel said. "Why didn't he have someone pull us over?"

"If we're coming home, why bother?" Greyson replied. "Quieter outcome, and fewer people involved all around. If he's as good as everyone assumes, then he already knows we've likely found something so explosive that we can't call him. Can't call for backup in Florida. Don't even trust other Hunter offices not to have been tainted by Zielinski along the way."

"SWAT teams going to arrest us at my place?" Rachel grinned.

"Only if we stop there first," Greyson grinned back. "More likely he's looking at the schedule, having a nice lunch, and asking someone with a black bag to open my front door so he can be seated on the couch when we walk in."

"He take all the files at that point, or will you fight him on it?" Rachel asked.

"If I trusted him, I'd let him have them," Greyson said.

"And thus, obviously, you don't," she nodded. "Who do we trust? Who do you trust to handle this?"

"Quinton Laux," Greyson smiled at her, watching her

face drift into confusion like a small mudslide trying to escape a hillside.

"Why him?" she stammered.

"He's not involved," Greyson said. "Except that he is, because he wants to solve a mystery about that chip."

"And you're going to hand him everything and hope he doesn't make copies while we're gone?" she pressed.

"Not going to tell him what it is." Greyson turned serious. "And I'm planning to make him a deal if he'll play."

"What?"

"I'll get him access to the chip itself," Greyson said. "If this represents that big of a technological jump, but one that he could replicate, he's rich. How many people would willingly burn the chance to be fabulously wealthy?"

"There's about thirty million bucks in the back of the car over there," Rachel pointed out. "Neither of us have actually listened to the evil fairy on our shoulder and slipped any of those certificates out and hidden them in the car."

"Oh, I've considered it," he explained. "Thought long and hard about it while you were asleep, as I figure you did when I was napping."

"That's fuck-you-money, Greyson," she nodded as they continued to amble, watching the dog finally get to the ball, woof at it once, and then happily tear off with it in her mouth.

"It is," he agreed. "Untraceable. Uncatalogued even now, because I don't want to know if you did slip one of them into your pocket. I've got enough pensions to get me where I need to go. You don't yet, so you have a much greater argument to have with yourself."

"How do you get over those things?" Rachel asked. "How did you, when you were my age and had something similar come up?"

"I was young and dumb," he replied. "Let me tell you

about this one place that might or might not exist, in a Central American country with a long history of antipathy to the old United States, going back way before I was born."

She glanced up at him and Greyson caught the nod in her eyes.

"So this gentleman in question was what the more lurid news organizations might have called a drug lord in the old days," Greyson said. "Once upon a time, back in the 1970s and 1980s, the US government went so far as to protect some of those folks, because their product was used to flood the black neighborhoods here with cheap crap, back at the time that the laws were changed to make the penalties for crack possession hundreds of times worse than cocaine. White people did coke. Blacks got hooked on crack, and racists like Olek Zielinski are not a new development in law enforcement by any stretch of imagination."

"Learned that in my ancient history class," Rachel grinned.

But he supposed it might be, to her. He'd been born in 2008. She didn't come along until 2035. Shit from 1985 might be as far away as the Civil War, at least to her. Back in the bleak days of a War on Crime that was a thinly-veiled War on Black People that had started before 1618 and never really been forced to subside until aliens landed and threatened to crack heads together.

"So I was sent in to remove said gentleman from his organization by whatever means I felt were most appropriate, as long as he was gone afterwards," Greyson continued.

"Extreme prejudice?" she asked tentatively.

"Oh, I supposed I could have kidnapped him, hauled him off to Switzerland, and offered him a deal," Greyson grinned now. "But that wasn't why they'd send in someone like me, you know?"

"Kill them all, make God sort them out?" she said knowingly.

"Something like that," Greyson said. "He was almost archetypal. Money arriving in suitcases and no bank would touch him, so he invested it in all sorts of tacky, expensive art. Or military grade hardware for his men. A string of houses and mistresses. The usual. And a bolt hole he would run to when trouble arrived. A panic room, if you will, except that it had a tunnel down and out the back, with a couple of guns, some body armor, and a briefcase filled with the same sorts of papers Zielinski had. There was a fast truck with armor plating at the other end of the tunnel, in a garage that didn't have any external connection to the main house, being down in the slums below."

"How'd you kill him?" she asked.

In the distance, the pup had gotten the ball back to the man with the stick, and was now madly racing after it again.

"Wired a bomb to the ignition of the truck," Greyson said. "Figured the armor would contain everything nicely so I wouldn't hurt too many innocent neighbors. Local Special Forces staged a raid for me. Mostly just a lot of shooting to get everyone's energy up. Sure enough, about five minutes later, a secondary explosion lit up the night."

"How much money was in that briefcase?" Rachel stopped and turned to him.

"About half again as much as ours," he said seriously. "And I burned it all. Mix of thermite and plastic explosives, with a claymore mine under the driver's seat."

"Would you make the same decision today?" Rachel asked.

He could tell she was having what a shrink might have called a crisis of conscience, but he didn't have any good answers. Greyson's entire life was really made up of secrets now.

"I'm not the one to judge, Rachel," he said. "Like I said, I was young and dumb then. And truly believed in what I was doing."

"Do you still?" she pressed.

"I believe in the job," he clarified. "It needs doing, just like you need someone to clean the streets and haul trash and recycling away. Zielinski and others let the job get away from them. They let themselves become more important than the laws they were supposed to enforce. When you do that, you start cutting corners, telling yourself whatever little lies comfort you, but eventually you either simply turn evil or you have to come clean. I never turned then. If I have secrets now, I'll deal with them. You'll do the same."

"Did any of what you just said have any value?" she asked after a second.

"Maybe," he laughed. "Vague pontifications from a tired cop can mean everything, or nothing. If you need to slip one or two into a pocket, I'm not going to stop you, as long as you leave me enough to burn Zielinski afterwards."

She started walking again and he followed. The only sound was that old pup woofing madly at the ball when she caught up with it, and then the sound of her claws whenever she crossed concrete getting back for another run.

He really didn't care what Rachel did. As long as he really could burn the man.

Greyson hadn't bothered telling her about a file he'd found clear at the back of one of the drawers while she'd been napping.

Upkins, D.

Just a small stack of photographs in it. He'd been in all of them.

Greyson had pulled the name tab off and stuffed it into a pocket while claiming one of them for himself and stuffing it into his pocket.

One photograph. Him and Denise, eating at that Ghanaian restaurant that had been one of their first dates.

What he couldn't tell was why Zielinski had kept it. Or what it meant. If that was all the man had, then Denise was probably safe. Or was it enough to suggest a much wider blackmail that didn't need to be in there?

Not something anybody needed to know about but him. And maybe Denise, when he saw her, but it would have to be someplace where it was just the two of them. Not even Redhawk got to know.

Or Rachel.

[28]

BOSTON

GREYSON IGNORED THE CHIRP OF OUTSTANDING messages and unheard voice mails as he finally turned his comm's access to the outside world back on. It would probably ring in a few minutes, too, but he wasn't about to answer.

Redhawk could wait.

Instead, he typed a quick message to Laux and hit send.

Available for a consult?

There, leave it vague and hopefully entice the man. It was mid-afternoon now and the storms they had been driving through all day had more or less come to Boston with them. Traffic into town wasn't all that bad, but Greyson marked that down to robots generally being better drivers than most of the humans he'd ever met.

Greyson had learned to drive on an ancient Fiat stick built before he was born and rebuilt several times by a bunch of semi-hillbilly redneck racers. They had a race every year, where the rule was you weren't supposed to spend more than $500 US on your car, back when that was a week's wages for some folks. Junkyard heaps and end-of-life things welded back together long enough for a day.

From there, the Army had taught him how to drive offensively as well as defensively.

Today, he just continued to let the robot drive the rest of the way in. Its reflexes were better than his would be right now, as tired as he was, and its decision-making was good enough, since it would do the predictable thing that all the other robots could react to appropriately.

Greyson wondered if he should take Rachel out to the west coast to meet the kids of those original weirdos, just so they could teach her what to do with two tons of steel in an emergency.

Capital! ETA? - QL

Greyson could almost see the smile on the man's face.

Newton, inbound, he typed.

I shall start the water boiling.

"What's so funny?" Rachel asked, so he showed her the screen, closing the announcement that Edgar Redhawk was calling.

"Gods, he's an even worse dork than you are, isn't he?" she rolled her eyes at him.

"Maybe," Greyson grinned and kept laughing.

"We still parking below and walking back up with everything?" she asked.

"Actually, my plan was to pay him to keep watch on the car after we put everything back in the trunk," Greyson replied. "Figure that's as safe as anything, and the rental system's radio won't be able to penetrate all the concrete and steel overhead, so they'll know the rough neighborhood but not the exact address until they come looking. Redhawk can't get any closer either, and then we walk out the front door of the grocery and catch a bus."

Her eyes got narrow.

"How are you going to burn Zielinski?" she asked.

"I have a couple of things in my pocket," he said. "Will pick up a couple more at the store on the way in. Then we swing by my place and I can have a shower and clean clothes. Pretty sure Redhawk will be waiting for us when we get there, but there's going to be an extra half-hour delay, so I'll eventually turn my phone back on and let him track me."

"Got it all worked out?" she asked.

"Not even remotely," he admitted with a grin, lest she think he was some sort of genius mastermind here. "Just not playing this one anywhere close to the playbook that either Redhawk or Zielinski are expecting. Hopefully I can keep them off balance."

"So if Redhawk's going to be there already, what are the chances I won't get a shower after this?" Rachel asked sidelong. "Wondering if I should keep a change of clothes at your place for emergencies or something."

He could only hope the woman was kidding. Teasing him, because Emmy would have questions if another woman's clothes showed up in the closet next to some of hers.

Cop/Alien erotica did not leave him with a good taste in his mouth. Hopefully just a mental kink the woman was after, and nothing physical she sought.

Please God, anything but that?

"You could call him now and have him swing by your place to get something," Greyson offered defensively, hoping everything here had mirth behind it.

"Once we surface," she decided from her tone. "Don't want to show up to the grand finale with a funk of two days in a car going."

He nodded and started to program a new destination into the system, then changed his mind and took over driving. They were only a few minutes away, if traffic held, and he'd rather not leave more in the system than he needed to.

Everything was going to be inspected by someone when this was all done. Greyson wanted to hang on to some of his secrets.

They dropped off the freeway and got to the parking garage with a minimum of fuss. All the way down and into a quiet corner.

It was quick work getting everything into the trunk, and then they walked back up a floor and got into the elevator.

"Tea's just steeping," a voice announced as they went back down a level.

Greyson took that as a good sign and they made their way back to the office where they'd met Laux twice before. Except that the room was dark and the office across the hallway was lit.

That turned out to be a much more pleasant, living room kind of space, with a funky, green couch dominating one wall, mismatched, overstuffed chairs in brown and gray, and a kitchenette bigger and nicer than the one Zielinski had. Or Greyson.

There was a large, ceramic pot of tea, with Chinese characters telling some story around the outside. Greyson didn't read the language, and didn't feel like snapping enough pictures for a translator program to handle the process for him.

Laux was dressed for church or something. A much nicer suit than he'd worn either time before. Just dark enough to be serious and sober, but it was still burgundy. The white silk shirt and cherry red silk tie should have looked gauche, but somehow made him look professorial.

Greyson could never pull off that look without feeling silly. Rachel might have the chops.

"Greetings, my interesting associates," Laux saluted them with his own mug as they entered.

And his smile was irrepressible, a glow of white teeth against his dark brown skin.

Greyson nodded and fixed two mugs of tea.

Laux had taken the brown chair, so Greyson sat on the farther end of the couch, nodding at Rachel to sit between them.

"And how may I provide assistance, Detectives?" Laux grinned at them.

"I'd like to leave the rental car here for a day," Greyson said simply. "And pay you a reasonable bribe to make sure that nothing happens to it until I could return."

"Reasonable?" the man perked up. "What's reasonable look like, Leigh?"

"I think we're about to blow the case wide open, Laux," he replied, sipping at a particularly good pu'er tea that was just at the right amount of chewy. "Three quarters of it, anyway. That last quarter remains complicated."

"How so?" Laux sat up sharply.

"From here, I'm going to have someone arrested, and then sweated," Greyson said in a cold, deadly voice. "I don't think he'll give me the address where that chip was made. I also don't think that the other officers working this case will be able to track it either."

"Where do I come in?" Laux asked.

"If we pull this off, they'll probably give us *carte blanche* to solve the rest," Greyson said, nodding to Rachel. "I'd like to bring you in as a special consultant in an official capacity of some sort, so you have hands-on with that chip."

Greyson figured it was like dangling a bottle in front of a recovering alcoholic, but he also didn't figure the man would object.

"And in trade?" Laux asked a little breathless.

"The car has some of the evidence I need to take my subject down, but none of it is actually related to solving this case," Greyson hedged. "He might want to cut a deal when he loses all that. About all he'll have left is the chip, so either he tells me how he did it and I get to tell you, or he doesn't and you try your luck at it."

Laux had stopped breathing. Greyson almost smiled at that, but he was too tired. Too angry. Too something.

He'd had to deal with Zielinski being a shit for too many years. Then sending assassins after him.

Greyson Leigh was feeling a little ugly right now.

"Why me?" Laux finally asked, having worked his way through a complicated decision tree of alternatives.

"You have all upside," Greyson said. "You play straight with me here and maybe I make you rich. Maybe just give you a one- to two-year head start on your competitors. Other folks are less trustworthy right now because the evidence I do have is going to ruin a few lives if it comes out."

"That makes us targets for more assassins," Rachel helpfully pointed out, causing Laux's eyes to get a little big.

But he also seemed to get the message that the car was a bomb. Maybe an armored SUV parked in a secret garage, waiting for someone to come along and use it.

After all, if that one man had stayed put in his bunker, he'd have probably been able to hold off those *Federales* for far longer than they wanted to dance.

But Greyson had been a hunter then, too. When it involved finding the right game trail and waiting for your prey.

Quinton Laux didn't have that look in his eyes. That one that said he'd be a problem. Part of it was a fear of what sorts of assassins someone might send after cops who had already successfully killed the first one.

Greyson assumed they'd use a bomb next time, if Zielinski had a chance to take a second shot at him.

Which was why Greyson Leigh was going to drop a whole ton of bricks on the man all at once.

"How long?" Laux finally asked.

"Twenty-four hours, at most," Greyson reassured him. "After that, someone will come back for it and we'll set up a password or something so you don't end up calling the cops if it is anybody but Rachel or me."

Laux took a longer sip of his tea. Chewed on it for a long moment as he worked his way through whatever stages of death matrix he had in his head, offsetting a little possible advantage now against a possible favor from a grateful Leigh later.

Didn't take him any longer than Greyson was expecting.

"I believe I can handle my responsibilities," the man said, holding out a hand for Greyson to shake. "Now what?"

Greyson leaned back and let the heat of the tea start to fill in some of that cold hollowness in his chest.

This had been the easiest part.

Now he just had to deal with Edgar Redhawk.

And Olek Zielinski.

Then finally Denise Upkins.

[29]

THE DANCE

RACHEL WATCHED HER PARTNER TRANSFER EVERYTHING he'd just bought at the grocery store out of the bag he had grabbed out of the car and into various pockets. Bottle of kombucha. Beef jerky. Stamps. Cheap lighter. Bag of trail mix. Today's newspaper. A thing of manila envelopes.

Mundane shit. Except for the suggestion that Greyson was maybe going to be mailing something to someone. Or several someones.

Given the contents of some of those files, she was a little hesitant to ask. There would be no good answers.

Lives were set to be utterly destroyed, but she still didn't know which way Greyson Leigh was going to jump, and that frightened her.

He was still acting like he was clinically depressed. Going out in a blaze of glory, as it were, taking everyone and everything down with him.

If it was Greyson.

Had the Phrenic somehow gotten control of their body again? Was that possible? Nothing anyone had ever said or written down on the species to talk about a Deathwalker had any useful details, except that they came apart in a few days.

But they were supposed to revert to base form when that happened, because the human didn't know how to control the body. Greyson seemed physically in charge. Emotionally he was in a different place.

A man with no fucks left to give.

She wondered if she should have ended up grabbing a page or two from the chicken fried steak box before they left everything behind. Rachel from a year ago, before Greyson Leigh, probably would have.

But she'd been partnered with Carlos Dominguez then, and that man was so bent he had to screw his pants on in the morning, it seemed.

Rachel Asher realized that she wanted to be an honest cop. One of the few that a man like Leigh would respect. If poverty was the cost, relative to men like Zielinski or Dominguez, that was acceptable.

After all, Zielinski had been living like a bum in a walk up, even when he had enough money in the freezer to buy the property he'd been living on and probably every other one within a couple of kilometers.

But he'd been a cheap man anyway. She remember that much. Bad suits. Sandwiches he brought from home instead of lunch out. Little things.

The rain around them had held off a little. Or maybe passed. Hard to tell. The skies were low and a darker gray promising pain later. The wind was a fierce hawk coming at them from the northwest as they started down the street.

"Call Redhawk now, if you want clothes," Greyson reminded her as they navigated that crowd of civilians possibly sneaking out early from a regular job to have a drink at a bar or something.

She didn't understand how office drones lived and kept their sanity, but she'd wanted to be a cop since she'd first written it in her diary at eight.

Rachel still had that diary, stored in a box at her parent's house.

She pulled out her comm and let it finally talk to the network again. Machine took a little while, possibly just being pissy, and then downloaded all the messages and missed calls she'd been avoiding for the last eighteen hours.

She dialed and Redhawk answered immediately.

"You two finally coming in?" he asked in a friendly-enough tone.

"Yup," Rachel replied simply. "Headed to Greyson's place so he can change and take a shower. Wondering if you had anybody that might swing by my apartment and get me a change of clothes, to save us a second trip?"

"Already have an overnight bag packed for both of you," he laughed. "Wasn't sure which place to break into, so I did both of them. Down the street from Greyson's in his favorite coffee shop right now. What's your ETA?"

"Hang on," she said, pulling the machine down so she could check bus schedules. "Maybe thirty minutes, including walking and wait time for the bus."

"Good enough," he said. "Looking forward to hearing all about it."

And then he hung up.

She stared at her comm for a long second, muttered a profanity under her breath, and stuffed it into a pocket.

"And?" Greyson asked.

"He was that far ahead of us both already," she said.

"No," Greyson said. "I made sure that it was obvious what we were doing, so he wasn't paying that close attention to all the other things we were doing."

Rachel shivered at his voice. Death might be jealous of that tone.

"Now what?" she asked.

"Now we go dance with the devil," Greyson replied.

[30]

EDGAR

PART OF HOW GREYSON STAYED IN SHAPE INVOLVED walking up and down the stairs, everywhere he went. He remembered stories about men like the old actor Kirk Douglas, who had done the same, and lived to be over one hundred, at a time when his life expectancy at birth had been about sixty.

Greyson liked the thought of a five decade bonus. Whether he used it to keep stomping on bad guys or took up some other hobby would remain to be seen.

So he walked up to his apartment instead of taking the lift. He'd already spotted at least one car down the street that was probably a couple of plain-clothes thinking they were invisible. He expected a few more.

That was why he'd hidden the rental.

Just because, he treated his door like it was fully locked and patiently undid all five before he opened it. Five was an unnecessary number, but he had felt like being an unnecessary person when he did it.

Not even a police ram would get through it, after what he'd done to the frame.

He smiled and pushed the door in, letting it swing all the way back to bang into the stopper and bounce off.

No carpet in here, just raw concrete floors that had been polished with a diamond wheel until they looked like marble. Rugs of various sizes instead.

The Murphy bed folded up against the wall, like he'd left it, with the table under it flipped down for Greyson to sit and read the news while drinking his coffee.

He looked at the faded mustard of the walls, almost a yellowed egg-shell, and decided that maybe Emmy was right and he needed something else. She'd suggested salmon, but Greyson hadn't been prepared to take that sort of a step.

Maybe he was now.

Couch and one chair in the middle, facing the windows that took up most of that wall. The one bookcase with all the things he hadn't been willing to hand to Liz to sell yet, but that was down from six such shelves two years ago.

Nobody needed physical books anymore. You could call up the entire collected wit and wisdom of the human race on your comm for a cheap price these days.

Greyson was just enough old-fashioned that he liked the smell of a book when he opened it. Wood pulp. Ink. Glue.

He'd spent way too much time in the county library as a kid. That smell always took him back to a simpler, happier place.

Redhawk was in the chair. Probably because it faced the door so he wouldn't leave much trace of his passage in here. Nobody else was with him.

That was good. Greyson had contained the niggling fear that Denise would be here. He needed his ducks in a row, not pretending to be drunk squirrels at a rave.

Redhawk first. Then Zielinski.

Then maybe Denise? Maybe not?

Too soon to tell.

Greyson stripped off his jacket and carried it to the cleaning bag. It didn't have a funk yet, but it would get there if he wore it for much longer.

Rachel would know that smell. He had no idea if Redhawk would, as well.

Not a test he wished to administer today.

"I need a shower," Greyson announced, pulling things from his pockets and unhooking the two holsters.

Redhawk nodded silently. He had a bag next to him that presumably had spare clothes for Rachel. Greyson wondered if he'd be able to tell from his closet what Redhawk had pulled out, and if he had returned it.

Greyson wanted to say he didn't care, but he'd be lying. He just had no fucks left to give, and that wasn't the same thing.

He just grabbed things from the dresser as he went by, stopping at the closet and pulling out a clean suit to wear.

The nicer one.

Not the one he would wear to take Emmy to the opera, or a museum, but maybe a nice dinner date uptown where the staff knew her by name because she entertained clients and business partners there regularly.

Greyson headed to the bathroom and closed the door behind him.

He needed a little time entirely vacant of people.

Greyson emerged thirty minutes later clean and shaved. Dressed to the sevens maybe, instead of the nines. Better than Zielinski deserved, but he wasn't doing this for that shitbird.

This was all a performance, and he was playing a character. Hopefully not Shakespeare, because as near as he could tell, everyone died when the Bard of Avon got rolling.

Maybe the fates would settle for him being Horatio? If this was Hamlet, and you could kind of squint and see that, it worked. Everyone important had died by the end of Hamlet. Mostly badly, too.

Only Horatio had emerged with mind and body intact. Even Rosencrantz and Guildenstern, slapstick duo that they'd been turned into much later, got the shaft.

Yeah, Horatio. He could work with that.

Rachel walked right by him into the bathroom and closed the door, Redhawk's bag in hand. He smiled at her, refreshed even enough to spend the evening with these people.

Greyson went to the kitchen and started assembling everything back into pockets. The snacks went into the outside pockets of the jacket. The envelope and stamps stayed on the table.

Both holsters.

Rather than start *that* conversation, he began the labor of making coffee. Water from the tap into the electric kettle. Hand-press from the drying rack where it lived most of the time. Filter from the cabinet shelf next to the honey. Beans from the freezer.

Greyson had learned a long time ago that roasted coffee beans that are frozen lasted a lot longer than sitting on the shelf. He generally went through them too fast for age to set in, but the Army had pounded some things bone deep. Their willingness to serve shitty coffee was close to the top.

Coconut cream from the refrigerator door. He wasn't a vegan or anything. Had just gotten hooked on the stuff during a—…let's call it a business trip to a place in southeast Asia where a young white boy like him had had no business being. And not everyone could digest cow's milk.

Water on to boil. Beans into the hand-cranked grinder, because he liked a fairly coarse result, and electric ones reduced them to powder.

Greyson assembled the hand press and pulled a mug

from the bottom shelf of the closest cabinet. Beans got ground and dropped into the top of the hand press.

Sometimes, he would put things into the mug directly, so they could dissolve when the hot water arrived. Collagen for joints. Maybe matcha tea powder. Whatever his body craved.

Right now, he wanted caffeine and heat.

Redhawk had stirred and risen. Greyson marked his approach by sound, smell, and the heat the man gave off, but maybe he was wound a little too tight right now.

"That almost looked like meditation in motion," Redhawk offered in a friendly voice.

"Tried Tai Chi Chuan once, but I didn't want to learn Mandarin," Greyson glanced back.

The water was hot enough, so he unplugged the kettle and poured the water over the grounds, stirring with his other hand as the slurry turned brown. Bubbles let him know that everything was still fresh.

Today, he was having a four. The press was filled almost to the top, just so the water would be the darkest and chewiest.

Redhawk was holding a to-go cup from the place down on the corner, but Greyson wouldn't have offered to share his expensive beans with the man anyway.

They were unindicted co-conspirators, not comrades.

He stirred until the water drained down to about the two level. Washed the stirrer and grab the plunger. Pressed the water the rest of the way through the grounds, then dumped grounds into the composting bin for the old lady on six who liked to grow blueberries and roses in pots, and used the grounds for her soil.

Add honey and stir to dissolve, listening to the sounds of the building. Rachel in the shower. Redhawk dead silent except for the occasional sip of coffee. Traffic down below on the street as people were headed home from a normal day of work, unaware of the dark things swirling around them.

If Greyson was doing his job, they would never have to know.

Half cup of coconut milk, because he figured he'd need the fat later to keep him going.

It was going to be a long, ugly night.

Both men returned to the living space when he was done, Redhawk in the chair, Greyson on the couch. The shower stopped. They waited in companionable silence.

She emerged a few minutes later, hair towel-dried and down. She almost always wore it in a tail or braid, so he tended to forget how long it was, or how much more she looked like a beautiful woman and less like a cop when she had it loose.

Her body and face turned men on. It was the job she did that left them cold and maybe running for the door. But then, most men didn't know how to deal with a woman who was tougher than they were, and probably smarter.

Their loss.

"Coffee?" he asked, holding out his mug like he did with Emmy.

She grabbed it and took a sip, but handed it back quickly.

"Yuck," she offered as her usual commentary.

He nodded and she sat next to him, already starting to braid her hair up and out of the way.

"What's your first step?" Redhawk asked finally.

"I have probable cause to arrest Olek Zielinski," Greyson said. "However, if we enter it into evidence or show it to a judge to swear out an arrest warrant, all hell breaks loose pretty damned fast."

"Why is that?" Edgar asked, leaning forward now, eye glittering with something. Maybe greed. Maybe revenge.

Maybe gas.

"Zielinski was blackmailing folks," Greyson replied.

Those eyes turned dead black now. Deadly black.

"You have his files," Redhawk said. It was not a question. "Does he have backups offsite?"

"Maybe, but I doubt it, considering everything that we retrieved," Greyson nodded to Rachel. "I'd like someone to take him into custody and haul him down to the Bureau like a regular prisoner. Throw him in a box for a while under the Official Secrets Act and then I'd like to have a conversation with the man. Just the two of us, plus whoever is on the other side of the mirror."

"Did he send the assassin?" Redhawk asked, maybe a touch confused now.

"Circumstantial evidence suggests that he did," Rachel jumped in now. "Nothing that will stand up in court, though."

"And you want to question him over...?" Redhawk asked.

"I think I can get a confession out of him," Greyson smiled. "At that point, everything else becomes irrelevant."

"Who was he blackmailing?" Redhawk asked, careful now.

"Just about everyone, near as I can tell," Greyson said. "Kwan and Owens close by, but there are a dozen other files filled with dirty secrets. I don't want them public, if we can avoid it."

Redhawk studied his face now, trying to read him.

Back when he'd been human, Greyson had known he had a poker face, not giving anything away. Now, he had such precise bodily control that he could probably go live in a casino at a card table and end up owning the place in a year.

If he cared.

About anything except revenge.

Redhawk pulled his comm and dialed.

"Yeah," he said simply to whoever answered. "Locate Olek Zielinski, the former captain of the local Hunter Bureau. He's probably at the hospital with Fred Jansen, or close by. Find him, and arrest him. Hard take down if he gives you any reason. Treat him like a common criminal, possibly armed, and haul him to the Bureau. Process him, fingerprint him, and drop him into the isolation cell. Yes, right now. I'll be there in a while to explain, but I want him taken out of circulation immediately. Call if you screw up anything and I need to have you fired. Am I clear?"

Long pause and Redhawk hung up, eyes never once leaving Greyson's face.

"I'm a little out on a limb here, Leigh," Redhawk said as he put his comm away. "It better be good."

"Oh, it is," Greyson smiled ominously. "You'll see."

[31]
OLEK

GREYSON HAD NEVER SPENT A LOT OF TIME DOWN IN the basement of the Bureau. If nothing else, Hunters either tended to find someone for the regular cops to arrest, or went in shooting and didn't have prisoners to arrest afterwards.

Sometimes, however, it was useful to put someone in a small, gray box, deep underground and let them stare at concrete walls for a while so they could contemplate their sins in privacy.

He didn't figure Zielinski had any introspective qualities to engage tonight, but the time spent in a cell would still do wonders for a control freak like Olek. Greyson smiled and considered what a small soul he might have.

He and Rachel were in the observation room. Redhawk was there with them. Parsons, too. The rest of the folks that might have joined them had been instructed to remain elsewhere, including the folks with emergency medical training, if Zielinski went and had a heart attack on them or something.

Parsons could call them back. If she wanted to.

Greyson watched Zielinski get delivered into the

interrogation room on the other side of the mirror and left in one of the two chairs still handcuffed in front. He was dressed in cheap blue chinos and a white sweater that had marinara stains on it, so they hadn't busted him all the way down to a prison jumpsuit.

Not yet, anyway.

Zielinski's face seemed pleasant enough, but that was a front. Greyson could almost smell the anger coming off the man in waves, like ozone.

That also brought a warm spot in Greyson's heart.

But then, turnabout was a bitch, wasn't she?

"You safe in there alone?" Rachel asked.

"You bet," he replied, but he still pulled out the nerve scrambler and palmstunner, handing them to her.

She slipped them into a pocket with a nod. Zielinski was handcuffed, but not bolted to the table. He could get up and walk around if he wanted. Or come across the table at Greyson and try to strangle him, maybe.

Greyson had six centimeters on the man, and didn't have the pot belly that Olek had started working on about four years ago, before getting serious about it down in Florida.

Rage might give the man strength, but Rachel could come in and kick his ass if Greyson needed it. Parsons was probably looking forward to it, when Greyson looked down and saw the heavy boots peeking out from the Captain's slacks. They looked remarkably like the ones Rachel wore every day, and the tall woman normally wore dressier shoes because she rarely went out in the field where they might get muddy.

Today might qualify as a special occasion.

"You folks pay attention," Greyson said. "I might ask you a question as he and I chat, so it would be nice if you answered quickly."

Redhawk moved to an electronics console that controlled

everything in both rooms and sat. He flipped a few switches and looked up.

"Recording is live," he said simply. "Medical scanners in Zielinski's cuffs are tracking his heart rate and other vitals, in case something happens. We're muted in here."

"Excellent," Greyson said cheerily. "Showtime."

He exited the observation room and nodded to the two beefy jailers standing outside the other door. Again, not that he needed them, but it was nice to have back up for once.

There had been too many instances of walking into a dark warehouse alone, with nothing but his pistol between him and somebody up to lethally-bad no good.

Or bad men in foreign countries with Death Warrants sworn out and signed by both the President and the Chairman of the Joint Chiefs.

Greyson opened the door and stepped in, closing it behind him and hearing the door lock itself.

Olek didn't bother to turn and look, but he'd be all about playing little power games right now, like the middle school bully he'd never outgrown. And there was a mirror taking up one whole wall that let the man see everything without moving his head.

Greyson walked around and pulled out the other chair, noting that the room was configured for two, so someone had taken the time to remove the third chair where a second interrogator normally sat.

Setting this up to dance, as it were.

Greyson sat, unable to help the shit-eating grin on his face as he stared at Olek's sourness. He was leaned back, while Olek was forward with his elbows on the table.

They held the tableau for perhaps a minute before Olek finally spoke.

"So you think you've got something on me, fucker?" he growled angrily. "Think I won't get you back?"

Greyson could have said something. Could have engaged this punk-ass little bitch in a verbal dance. Olek had probably spent the last hour planning for such a scenario, and the last forty years training for it.

Greyson wasn't feeling like playing nice.

The only better time to kick a man than when he was down was when he wasn't looking.

Greyson reached into an inner pocket and pulled a piece of paper from where he'd hidden it in his wallet earlier. While Rachel slept.

Nobody used Imperial measurements anymore, but it was what had been a four by six inch photo when Greyson was a kid. The machines that printed photographs still spit them out at the odd size.

He put his wallet away and reached into his pants pocket where he kept his change, pulling out the cheap lighter he'd picked up earlier.

Greyson set the image down on the metal table between them just long enough for Olek to identify it with a blink of surprise, before Greyson picked it up again and set it on fire before the old cop's hands could reach for it.

The old paper and the inks seemed happy to ignite, as it went up pretty fast.

Greyson still hadn't spoken, his face turning serious with concentration as he worked on not burning himself. Olek had a bead of sweat over his left eyebrow when Greyson looked up.

He dropped the burning picture on the table again and leaned back as it went up. Olek did the same, possibly fearing that his old, ratty sweater might catch.

Greyson noted a fire extinguisher in a corner, if he decided he needed to put Olek out.

Another long pause.

"Where'd you find that?" Olek asked in a voice that strove for braggadocio and settled for reedy and thin.

"Two Oh Seven," Greyson replied simply.

Greyson watched the little light bulb come on in Olek's eyes. They both knew what 207 signified. On a variety of levels.

Olek fell silent. Greyson watched the man chew iron nails with his lips closed, possibly spalling enamel off his teeth as he ground them.

"And then we went out to a celebratory dinner," Greyson mentioned off-hand before raising his voice. "Rachel, what did I eat when we hit that one diner after?"

"Chicken fried steak," her radio voice filled the room with warmth and a hint of coquettish giggles. She even added just a shade of southern twang, like a Texas belle.

Olek didn't manage to hide a flinch fast enough for Greyson to miss it.

"Chicken fried steak," Greyson repeated slowly, savoring the words like he had that meal last night. "Could have had the mashed potatoes and diced veggies, plus the little cherry turnover thing for dessert, but I'm not like you, Olek. I went all in on the breakfast instead. Eggs over easy. The really runny kind you mop up with some warm, sourdough toast because you want to clean the plate and enjoy life. Hash browns extra crispy with extra salt. And pork sausage and bacon gravy. Damn, but that was a nice breakfast. Thank you for suggesting it."

Zielinski might have growled under his breath. It was hard to tell. Probably quiet enough that the microphones in here didn't pick it up. Maybe it was just in his eyes.

"You think you got it all figured out, punk?" Olek finally responded in a low, dangerous voice.

Almost as deadly as Greyson right now.

But only almost.

"I don't have to, Olek," Greyson replied.

The picture had stopped burning. It was nothing but a pile of crumbled ash, like bacon badly overcooked the way his mom had always insisted on when Greyson was a kid. Dry and crumbly. Lacking passion. Also like her.

Greyson tapped a finger on the table next to the ashes, drawing the other man's eyes down.

"I've got you other ways," Greyson continued. "It's not necessary to pin an assassination attempt on you, although when Jansen wakes up and finds out that your ass is going down hard, he might want to cut a deal with me."

Again, that growl. That flinch that was never more than a twitch of the eyes.

"You understand, Olek," Greyson decided to stick the knife in and twist it a little. Nick him again. Not like he didn't owe this shitbird for a lot of things. "Buyer's remorse. Maybe he can say he thought it was all in fun and nobody told him that he'd be indictable in a conspiracy to commit murder of a Metropolitan Law Enforcement Agent. That's one of the few capital crimes still on the books, isn't it?"

"He won't talk," Olek muttered.

"He doesn't have to," Greyson said. "I've got more on him than you had on me, when you got me fired and blackballed. Talking is what might keep him out of a small, concrete box for the rest of his life. Like the one next to you down the hall."

It was like goading the bull with a red cape. Flash it and hide. Motion and stillness.

Taunt the fucker into making a mistake because he thinks size, mass, and motion mean something in this game.

Greyson had spent the whole drive home thinking about Olek Zielinski and the twisted contents of those files. The lives that might be ruined if any of it came out.

The year he had spent eating cut-rate udon, listening to

his classical music, and drinking the cheap synth whiskey while he recovered from the PTSD of his entire life.

Watching this son of a bitch walk out of the drizzle that day last fall and dangle something in front of him. Something Greyson had realized he really did want back.

Yeah, he owed Olek Zielinski the sword that the toreadors used, hidden in the cape.

"What do you want?" Olek asked.

Greyson had watched the man walk himself all the way through the stages of death as they both breathed slowly.

"I want to know the how, Olek," Greyson replied.

"The how."

"The why is pretty obvious to anyone with the sense God gave a goose," Greyson said. "That chip is the only piece that I haven't got solved at this point, but I also haven't been engaged in that side of the case. After I'm done with you here, I'll go have a chat about being made Lead Investigator. With your head on a stick, I'm pretty sure Parsons will be amenable."

"That's all you think I've got to trade?" Zielinski asked.

Greyson reached out again and tapped the table next to the crumbled pile of dead bacon.

"It's the only thing I want," Greyson sneered at the man.

Olek refused to take the bait.

"I can do a lot of things when I walk out of this room, Olek," he managed to reply without letting the snarl into his voice. The toreador's sword. "I can hand all those files over to Parsons or maybe Upkins, since this office shouldn't investigate itself, and let someone else handle it. Given what I have, you're never getting out of jail short of a pardon from Upkins or one of her successors."

He smiled at Zielinski. Pure, shit-eating grin again.

"Two: I can tell Parsons that I don't have anything at all on you," Greyson continued. "Nobody's seen it but me and

Rachel. What would happen if I told the entire world that I had burned all those files, destroying everything and they were free from you? With nothing to hold you, Parsons kisses you on both cheeks and you are free to walk out the front door upstairs and get on with your life."

He paused a beat.

"How long until someone starts sending killers after you, Olek?"

There. First blood. The taunted bull has charged, but they focus on color, charging the cape. The man or woman holding the cape slashes at the stupid beast. At least that's what he remembered from the cartoons when he was a kid.

Olek was bleeding, at least metaphorically. And they both knew it.

Given the location, Zielinski might never make it back to Florida to pick up whatever emergency go-bag he had packed. Maybe he had a spare up here in Boston against such emergencies? Could he make it to a bank and his safety deposit box alive?

Greyson wouldn't interfere. Olek Zielinski was a private citizen now. There were no known threats against his life, so he didn't need police protection.

And they both knew it.

"So we come back to the how," Greyson continued, as if nothing had occurred. "You didn't design that Synth Chip. Nor manufacture it. The gun's easy. After all, lots of cops keep highly-illegal ghost guns at home, don't they?"

Another slash. Death of a thousand paper cuts was going to be the game, but only because literally tying Olek down and either waterboarding him or doing the ancient Chinese water torture was illegal.

Greyson wasn't going to inquire about the ethics of it today.

"And the perp was just a middle-aged nobody with the

right fetish, wasn't he?" Greyson asked. "Plug him in on the right day and bang, he makes the evening news for killing a couple of cops before a Heavy Response Team takes him down."

Long beat this time.

"You ready to talk yet, or should I start burning files?" Greyson asked. "I'll do them one at a time, so each of your enemies is free. Then I'll call them personally and let them know."

"Do you even care?" Olek growled.

Greyson considered it.

"No," he replied. "You could have lived a long and angry retirement down in that dump in Southport. Gone fishing with your buddies. Played D&D with the local police chief and his wife. None of it would have bothered me at all, because we'd made a deal, you and I. You went away forever and I didn't hunt you. You broke your end of the deal, Olek. So now you're mine to destroy. I'm looking forward to it."

He didn't mean for the way his voice dropped down to a ragged, rusty knife blade. Or the heat that boiled up from his belly, like a dragon's fire about to ignite that cheap cotton, marinara-stained sweater and turn Olek into a torch.

Olek Jan Zielinski appeared to finally discover fear, from the way his eyes got big for a moment. Like maybe he'd thought that he was protected. Insulated from anything anyone could do to him.

Except that the insulation had been hidden in a brass ashtray numbered 207, after the Hunter's badge that had been melted down and recast by someone.

It was gone now, and the cold was going to start seeping in.

"So the best you'll offer me is life?" Zielinski asked. Again, it was probably meant to sound tough, but it came out weak and a little frightened.

"No," Greyson replied with a shake of the head. "The best I'll offer you is your life. You get to tell me about that chip and how it got into your hands. Then you can tell Parsons all the details she needs to know about how and why you decided to kill me and Rachel, so that she has a reason to take you into protective custody, and then make sure they put you in a medium security prison somewhere in isolation instead of putting you in General Population and telling the other convicts you used to be a cop. But that's tomorrow. Let's talk about how you got your hands on an illegal Synth Chip."

For the longest time, Greyson didn't think the man would break. That maybe Olek Zielinski had enough intestinal fortitude to take his chances with the shitstorm that would erupt when all that blackmail became public.

Sure, Kwan and Owens would be permanently ruined. A lot of cases would have to be reviewed and probably a good number of convictions set aside after certain prosecutors were added to the list next to the former Police Commissioners.

If the system was broken, it had to be repaired. Greyson had considered how many innocents might be in prison right now because Zielinski had been able to lean on a District Attorney with money and kink issues. But at the same time, it was more likely that too many guilty had walked free for the same reasons instead.

He'd start after them tomorrow.

But something in Greyson's eyes seemed to get through to the man. Seemed to convince him that Greyson Leigh wasn't playing games anymore.

This wasn't the cat toying with the mouse. This was a nail just seated into a 2x4 awaiting the hammer.

So Olek talked.

Greyson leaned back and listened.

[32]

QUINTON

GREYSON HADN'T THOUGHT HE'D BE ABLE TO CONVINCE Quinton to emerge into the real world, but the man was bribable. All it took were the technical schematics of the Synth Chip, once Parsons had ordered Forensics to provide Greyson a copy.

Black Fab, just like Greyson had figured at the start. And one that knew just how dangerous the chip they'd made was, because near as Greyson could tell, they had shut the operation down as soon as they handed it over to Zielinski. Torn the facility apart and sold off the various machines on the second-hand market, leaving an empty warehouse stripped to the walls when a team of Hunters had arrived.

Gone.

Greyson would have felt better, except that the people who'd made the chip were still out there somewhere. Right now, angry accountants were tracing money in and out of the building, trying to find the perpetrators, but the folks involved had gotten a good head start and were already experts at hiding from the authorities.

But that wasn't Greyson's problem. Nor his case. He'd

handed them Olek Zielinski with a full-enough confession and a pretty pink bow in what was left of his hair.

Tonight, he was celebrating. Sort of.

If it was a real party, he'd have Emmy here, but this was still too much of a cop thing, so it was just him, Rachel, and Quinton, plus a promise from Parsons that she'd honor this expense report. But then, Greyson had promised to destroy the files rather than let the Bureau or the government have them.

Steaks. The good kind, where you got a half or maybe two-third of a kilo of prime rib, crusted with salt and cooked medium rare. Horseradish shavings in cream. Semi-mashed potatoes with all the usual toppings hand-mixed in. Asparagus spears cooked in real butter.

Greyson had skipped lunch so he could order himself a cherry turnover as one last *fuck-you* to Olek and his box of chicken fried steak frozen dinner filled with untraceable money.

Rachel was having a small dish of chocolate ice cream with caramel drizzled over it. Quinton was sipping a glass of port and occasionally reaching for the decaf coffee.

It was late, but this place had a bar attached so the restaurant didn't usually close until after ten.

Greyson took a bite of the turnover and savored the taste of revenge.

"So can you replicate it?" Rachel asked Quinton in between bites of her own.

"Can I?" the man said. "Absolutely. They did a few things differently from how I would have, but they were also creating a ticking bomb and they knew it. My design adds a few extra safety precautions and leaves off that nasty emotional filter your cop friend had them add. That was just evil."

Greyson had to agree. It was one thing to let them see the

outside world and add all that rich detail and setting as an overlay, but Olek had been poking at parts of the brain responsible for fear and aggression.

Quietly, so that you didn't realize it. The system just told you that were on a secret mission to create a Mass Casualty Incident and then emotionally prepared you to walk into a crowd and start shooting random innocents that happened to be in your way.

"So what do you plan to do with yours?" Greyson asked as he finished his last bite and reached for his own coffee.

Quinton fixed them both with a look that Greyson was pretty sure his own mother had taught the man. That *I-can't-believe-you-said-that* look that was midway between an angry huff and a sarcastic eyeroll.

"Sell them on the black market," he said pointedly, dropping his voice to barely above a whisper. "And yes, Detectives, I am aware that Synth Chips without the body cutout are completely illegal in almost all jurisdictions. Might I remind you that depending on how one wished to interpret things, somewhere between eighty and one hundred percent of what I do is probably illegal in the Eastern Metroplex?"

"Less than one hundred," Rachel spoke up. "You've been aiding law enforcement authorities to solve a crime. Pretty sure that's not currently illegal."

Everyone laughed at that one.

Greyson focused on the man.

"As long as nobody gets hurt, I don't care," he told Quinton. "Not my department. Not my cases. I was only on this one because of Zielinski trying to kill me. Pretty sure that if me being targeted hadn't suggested a leak in the Bureau, none of us would have been involved."

"Just so, Detective," Quinton said, still a little huffy before relenting. "But that doesn't change much. Because of your help, I can make a whole bunch of money this year, until either the chips get popular enough that they decide to change the laws, or some bad apples start making killer designs again and the government has to really crack down hard enough that I pull up stakes and walk away."

"I'd ask if you wanted a legitimate job, but the background checks they'd make you go through probably wouldn't be worth it," Greyson said. "Nor the pay cut."

"Certainly not the pay cut," Quinton laughed. "Even with the bribes I pay, I make way more than a Detective/Hunter does, Greyson."

"Well, with your permission, I'd like to keep you in my contacts list, Quinton," Greyson replied. "Never know when I might need an expert like you on case. Maybe I can make you rich again."

"Looking forward to it, Detective," Quinton smiled.

"Good," Greyson said simply. Dessert done, he rose abruptly. "You two stay and have a pleasant evening. I'm going to pay the bill and then go home and sleep for a day."

Rachel caught his hand before he could get far.

"Hey," she said simply. "Before you decide you have no fucks at all left to give, just remember that ya done good here. I don't know any other cops that would have destroyed all that blackmail. Nor mailed those bearer instruments to a variety of charitable organizations anonymously. You're a good cop, Greyson Leigh. And a good man. Keep that in mind."

Greyson blinked. For a moment, he wondered if he'd start crying right here in the restaurant, but he held it together with a gruff "Thank you" as he staggered off to where the waitress was approaching him with a bill.

Dinner for three didn't even run as much as he'd expected, but that was fine. It was Parsons's money when he turned in the report in a few days.

Right now, he just wanted to go home and let it all go. Even a day of chasing down leads after all of Zielinski's confession hadn't been enough time to recover from the last week.

Now he wanted to rest.

[33]

DENISE

GREYSON WALKED UP THE STAIRS TO HIS APARTMENT with a measured tread. Now that Zielinski was finally gone for good, he had a lot of thinking to do. Did he really want to keep doing this job? Keep getting his hands dirty and his boots bloody from wading through all the crap that this world could put out?

Rachel had been on the mark about no fucks left to give, except that he had found in the last few days that he did have a few. A man with nothing left would have handed over all that stuff to the Metropolitan's office and hoped that they would end up more honest than Zielinski. Or mailed it to the major news bureaus to run with, just so he could watch lives implode on the evening news with a highball glass in one hand and a snarl in his heart.

Maybe gone and bought himself a private island somewhere with all the money Olek had left him. Just lay on the beach and sip fancy rum drinks while being fanned by pretty girls.

He already knew that something like that would get old about two days in. Greyson Leigh was a seeker. A

243

Detective/Hunter. It was a job almost perfectly suited to his mind, his life, and his soul.

Somebody might as well get a benefit out of all that corruption. If Greyson had shown some of his otherwise private political leanings with the places he had mailed his packages, that was between him and God. And God supposedly loved everyone, so Greyson figured he was on safe ground rescuing kittens and funding women's shelters. Let them invest the money as they figured would do them the most good.

He was tired. Bone tired. Soul tired.

Greyson approached his door and unlocked everything patiently, as he did all things.

He opened it and smelled her perfume before he could even see her, but he was a Detective/Hunter. That was his job.

Emmy didn't wear that scent. And wouldn't be in his apartment when he wasn't there. Not that he hadn't offered her a key, but her only interest was him. If he was busy, she already had a life that involved carving out time to see him.

Greyson pushed the door the rest of the way open and looked in to see Denise sitting on the couch, quietly waiting for him. Her reader was resting to one side, so she'd been here a while.

He stepped across the threshold and closed the door behind him, taking a moment to reset all the locks before he turned to stare at the Metropolitan of the Eastern Metroplex.

"When you rekey the door, send me the invoice," she began carefully. "Redhawk had a spare key made when he was here. I have it with me, but you'll feel better returning everything to what it was before all this happened."

He grunted and took off his longcoat, hanging it on the hook beside the door. The boots went next.

For the hell of it, Greyson took his jacket off as well as he walked over to the kitchen chair and hung it across the back. The shoulder holster and palmstunner were next and he put them on the counter where they always went. Comm and wallet as well.

It was almost like he was alone in here. If he closed his eyes and dreamed hard enough.

Or clapped louder, because Tinkerbell would die otherwise.

Greyson turned to Denise and drank her in.

Fifty-five. Dark skin the color of old wood that had been polished clean. Brown eyes staring calmly back at him, maybe with a smile in them. Hair in loose ringlets but all black, even though he knew better.

She was dressed like she'd come here from the office. Whether that meant somewhere in Boston or maybe she'd quietly caught the bullet train up was irrelevant. She was here, and dressed for business, rather than seduction.

That was good. He wasn't entirely sure how he'd react if she'd poured him a glass of wine and put on some quiet jazz before he arrived.

Rachel had been right about his humor. And his direction.

Not many fucks left to give, even for Denise.

He pulled a heavy breath deep into his lungs and let it go, wondering if this was still Act Three or finally the denouement.

She had the couch, so he moved to the chair, settling into it about midway back. Not up where he might leap to his feet. Not back where he could put his feet up and nap.

"Hello, Denise," he said as casually as he could force right now.

It was close to midnight, and he'd been moving for four days, not counting catnaps. Grumpy only described his humor in the sense that it pointed in the right general direction.

"Hello, Greyson," she said, leaning herself back some.

She'd been poised when he walked in, but he wasn't sure if that was poised to jump up and kiss him, or to bolt.

He studied her for one long, last moment before this conversation started.

"To what do I owe the honor?" he finally asked.

She flinched a little at his tone, but she'd broken into his apartment and waited for him to return from his team's celebration of a successful conclusion on a number of different fronts. An assassination attempt. A corrupt Hunter. Another one, anyway.

God only knew how many were still around. Greyson had a feeling that everyone in the department was about to have accountants crawling up their asses starting tomorrow.

When he was a young cop, all of a decade ago, one of the oldest salts still around had used a term that had stuck with him. The man was a desk sergeant who had been allowed to stay on duty until he celebrated his fiftieth year in uniform. The man had been born in 1974, which felt like the Dark Ages these days.

Josh had called them "Blue Jean Cops" because they never understood how to hide shady money. Went out and bought expensive clothes and designer jeans before moving up to the sorts of fancy suits that Dominguez had collected. Or art and expensive cars. Antique firearms. Mistresses of every color, although usually all the same shape.

Greyson expected a lot of angry accountants going through people's drawers and closets soon but he wasn't worried.

He was busy saving kittens and funding women's shelters. Nothing at all on him, and he hoped Rachel was smart enough not to touch anything she might have pocketed for another few years.

Greyson didn't think Rachel had. She was trying too hard to wash the taint of Dominguez off her skin and her career. Replacing it with Greyson Leigh might be an improvement.

And it might not.

He watched Denise process his words. And the complicated emotions in his eyes. Finally she drew a breath.

"I asked both Rachel Asher and Redhawk," she said. "Neither of them knew the answer, so I suppose that's good."

Silence stretched.

Greyson watched her silently, unwilling to answer the question until she actually asked it.

"Did Zielinski have a file with my name on it?" she finally asked in a pained voice.

Only someone at least a little bent would even have to worry about something like that. There hadn't been a file on Greyson Leigh. Nor on Rachel Asher, but Greyson put that down to her not being important enough, since she'd been a mentee of Carlos Dominguez.

Without those two Phrenic, Ethen and Zaborra, Rachel might have drifted far enough to warrant her own file by now.

Greyson wondered what Denise thought someone might have on her.

"He did," Greyson replied quietly, letting it dangle like that.

She deflated. That was the only word Greyson could think of to describe the way she sagged in on herself, spine hunching and shoulders twisting inwards.

"But there wasn't much in it," Greyson completed the thought after a moment.

Her eyes came up with a gleam he could only describe as *hope*.

Greyson waited, while Denise composed herself and drew her own heavy breath.

"When it came time to make him go away, he suggested that it would be in my best interest to leave him alone," she said. "Without saying what blackmail evidence he might be willing to unleash if I didn't."

"Owens and Kwan are sleeping much easier tonight," Greyson nodded. "Or will be when they hear the news. You should never let either of them anywhere near a public job again, let us say."

"That bad?" she asked diplomatically.

"Worse than you probably imagine, if you have to ask, Denise," Greyson answered.

Greyson drew a breath and leaned forward a little.

"Rachel didn't know much because I went through it while she was asleep and hid it from her," he said. "Wasn't much, as a matter of fact, so I can't draw any useful conclusions and neither could anyone else, if they had managed to see it before it got destroyed. Nobody will."

She sagged again, but this time it was relief. Her eyes fell with her head before she lifted both up and fixed on him.

"What was it?" she asked, relief and fear warring with each other.

He studied her now. Saw the woman she had been once upon a time. Saw the woman she had turned into. Maybe only a little bent from her reaction, but there had been a file with her name on it in Zielinski's cabinet.

"Pictures," Greyson said simply.

Her eyes got a little twitchy in ways that she wasn't fast enough to hide. He wondered what she might have done that then might have gotten immortalized.

Confessions without ever speaking, like Rachel had done to him.

Latency, as Quinton Laux might have called it. The things there, but not seen.

"Most of them were pictures of us," Greyson added, dropping that into the silence like a rock into the mud at the edge of a still pond.

Like when he'd been a kid, an eternity ago.

"I burned them all first, before moving on to the more interesting things," Greyson continued.

She hadn't moved. Might have turned to stone for all she was breathing right now.

"Pictures of us?" she asked in a voice striving mightily to sound normal.

Wasn't going to fool anyone but they were the only people to hear them. The only two that mattered.

Greyson nodded, wishing that this had been the sort of scene where he'd gone ahead and fixed himself a highball of the synth whiskey to drink.

"I destroyed them all," he assured her again, eyes heavy as he watched her.

"When were they?" she asked.

"Back when we were maybe an item," Greyson replied. "Zielinski apparently had his eye on you, but he was already blackmailing everyone, so I figure it was just an insurance policy."

"You," she said. "Why?"

"There are many things you never learned about my past, Denise," Greyson offered. "You might have a high-enough security clearance these days to read some of them, but you're probably better off not knowing what I used to do for the Army."

"That bad?"

"I was an assassin, Denise," he said flatly. "Not everything I did would pass muster these days. Less so with the Merchant's Guild looking on. Better to let those things be."

"And Zielinski thought that just the association of your name with mine would destroy me?" she asked.

"People would ask questions," Greyson offered now. "I would become a brush they could use to tar you, when you go on and run for President, or maybe become Secretary-General. Things you'd want shut up, so you might have to engage folks that did things. Things even Edgar won't do for you."

She flinched at that, but Greyson supposed he had a much better understanding of a man like Edgar Redhawk than she did.

Denise was just a politician. Edgar was a killer, like Greyson. He just was willing to wear a tie.

Denise studied his face, looking for some softness he supposed. Wasn't there. Hadn't been, even before Ethen came along and changed everything.

"Destroyed," she murmured, as if understanding that he had gone beyond just burning a dozen photographs.

"Destroyed," Greyson echoed.

"And now?" she asked.

"Water under the bridge," he said harshly.

Greyson didn't want to hurt her. She was one of the most amazing women he'd ever met. Her and Emmy were of a type. Driven. Smart. Funny. Gorgeous.

Emmy had all her various companies and investments, a never-ending sequence of meetings to buy or sell some fragment. Maybe buy three companies and consolidate them into a new thing that could do something to revolutionize some industry. Then she'd sell it off to new investors and make her percentages on the deal.

Emmy didn't keep Greyson around on the stage either, but he did clean up well and could squire her around town to various events where she needed a Plus One to look even better than she normally did.

Denise Upkins dated retired jocks and famous actors. Other people at her level of wealth and fame.

The beautiful people.

She didn't need a broken down mutt of a former assassin with secrets anywhere near her life. Not then. Not now.

"Have you ever wondered—..." she started to say, but he interrupted her.

"That was six years ago, Denise," he snapped. "We made the right choice then for your career and mine. You and I had been an item, but that stopped right after Christmas of '51, as you should recall. My background has always been far too sketchy for a prominent pol like you to have off to one side. I might have blown your chance to be Metropolitan and we'd have had that schmuck Jovanon instead. There is nothing to be gained from digging all that back up again today. Nothing."

Harsh words, but he had to protect her. Even from herself.

She was edging over into maudlin now.

Into *Might-Have-Been* territory. He wouldn't have it.

Something like that only got you long nights drinking cheap synth whiskey and wondering where you went wrong and how it might have all turned out, *but-for-that-one-thing*.

Greyson had seen those sorts of thoughts destroy too many lives.

Slapping her with an open palm might have hurt less right now, but better to rip that bandage off all at once.

After a moment, she closed her open mouth and maybe ground her teeth a little too much.

Denise Upkins, *Her Honor* the Metropolitan of the Eastern Metroplex, rose silently and remembered her reader before she took a step. She stared at him for a long moment; hurt, surprise and anger all at war with each other in her eyes.

Tears, too, maybe, but they'd be unshed here.

Never in public, where someone might see them. Might blackmail you with them.

Later, after she was back at the hotel room she'd no doubt gotten as a backup against not staying here tonight. She'd cry there, alone in the privacy of her own thoughts.

That was the promise her face made now as she moved to the door and stopped, methodically unlocking each one.

Greyson didn't stand. That would make it too easy to ask her to come back. To take her in his arms and hold her again, so they could both cry about things that never were.

He remained sitting, grinding his own teeth and trying not to snarl at himself as a damned fool.

Denise opened the door and held it as she turned and stared at him, perhaps that fabled *one last time* they talk about in the movies and good books.

"I'm sorry, Denise," he finally said to her, studying her poised like a statue that one of the masters might have carved on his best day. "It's for the best."

That was all he could think of to take the sting out of the conversation they could never have. Not even in another decade or three after she was out of office and fully retired from public life.

Because he wasn't Human anymore.

Something got through, because she nodded, a compact motion involving everything above her belly button. No words, just that jerk that encompassed her whole torso.

She walked out the door, pulling it shut behind her.

And out of his life, but it was for the best, at least for her.

For all of them.

Greyson rose after a time.

It was still dark outside and he hadn't fallen asleep, but he'd indulged, just this once, in a fit of *might-have-beens*, wondering about the sorts of happily-ever-afters they might have been able to carve out.

He staggered to the kitchen and pulled the whiskey and a highball glass down from the cabinet, pouring himself three fingers instead of his normal one.

Greyson studied the caramel liquid as he swirled it. Good sipping whiskey, with just the right mix of peat, smoke, and sweetness behind it that you should always consume it at room temperature in slow, careful sips that let the flavor bloom on your tongue.

He tilted his head back and shot the whole thing down, letting the harsh fire fill the hollowness that was his soul. The cabinet door stared back at him blankly, but he didn't have much to say to it or anyone else.

Greyson opened his wallet and pulled out a picture he'd hidden in there earlier, when he'd added the rest to the burning trashcan behind an abandoned building on the edge of an industrial zone.

He stared at the photograph.

The two of them, holding hands across a table in a particular Ghanaian restaurant, the first time he'd taken her out to dinner. First dates were always a movie, or a museum. Food left too many chances to make a fool of yourself in front of someone you desperately wanted to impress.

The shooter had been a pro, framing everything in such a way that Greyson thought he might be able to walk to the exact spot on the sidewalk tomorrow and stand where the man had paused, snapped, and kept walking while two silly lovebirds stared into each other's eyes and smiled.

And then gone their separate ways, because having him in the picture would have cost a woman like Denise the chance to do the one thing she'd been aiming at for most of her adult life.

She'd been a good Metropolitan. Would continue to be,

until maybe she ran for President of the United States, or possibly Secretary-General of the World Council.

Denise didn't need all the issues that would come of having her romance with Greyson Leigh dragged out into the light by folks who were compelled to keep asking questions until they had answers.

Greyson Leigh, ex-US Army assassin, didn't have any good answers.

And all he could do right now was indulge in a useless round of *might-have-beens*.

So he stared at that picture. He could remember the night vividly, but he could not remember ever being that happy. He had been, from the smile on his face.

Greyson poured himself another two fingers and went back to that warm spot on the couch where she'd been sitting to sip it and remember.

It wasn't like he was going to get any sleep tonight.

ABOUT THE AUTHOR

Blaze Ward writes science fiction in the Alexandria Station universe (Jessica Keller, The Science Officer, The Story Road, etc.) as well as several other science fiction universes, such as Star Dragon, the Dominion, and more. He also writes odd bits of high fantasy with swords and orcs. In addition, he is the Editor and Publisher of *Boundary Shock Quarterly Magazine*. You can find out more at his website www.blazeward.com, as well as Facebook, Goodreads, and other places.

Blaze's works are available as ebooks, paper, and audio, and can be found at a variety of online vendors. His newsletter comes out regularly, and you can also follow his blog on his website. He really enjoys interacting with fans, and looks forward to any and all questions—even ones about his books!

Never miss a release!
If you'd like to be notified of new releases, sign up for my newsletter.

http://www.blazeward.com/newsletter/

Buy More!
Did you know that you can buy directly from my website?

https://www.blazeward.com/shop/

Connect with Blaze!

Web: www.blazeward.com
Boundary Shock Quarterly (BSQ):
https://www.boundaryshockquarterly.com/

ABOUT KNOTTED ROAD PRESS

Knotted Road Press fiction specializes in dynamic writing set in mysterious, exotic locations.

Knotted Road Press non–fiction publishes autobiographies, business books, cookbooks, and how–to books with unique voices.

Knotted Road Press creates DRM–free ebooks as well as high–quality print books for readers around the world.

With authors in a variety of genres including literary, poetry, mystery, fantasy, and science fiction, Knotted Road Press has something for everyone.

Knotted Road Press
www.KnottedRoadPress.com